FIC
HUNTER

HWLCFN

W9-DJH-377

R0177690097

What's left us : stories and a novella

What's Left Us

LITERATURE AND LANGUAGE DIVISION
LITERATURE INFORMATION CENTER
THE CHICAGO PUBLIC LIBRARY
400 SOUTH STATE STREET
CHICAGO, ILLINOIS 60605

What's

POLESTAR BOOK BUBLISHERS
Vancouver

Left Us

Stories
and
a Novella

Aislinn Hunter

Copyright © 2001 by Aislinn Hunter

All rights reserved. No part of this publication may be reproduced or transmitted in any form or by any means, electronic or mechanical, including photocopying, recording or by any information storage and retrieval system now known or to be invented, without permission in writing from the publisher.

Polestar Books and Raincoast Books gratefully acknowledge the support of the Government of Canada through the Book Publishing Industry Development Program, the Canada Council and the Department of Canadian Heritage. We also acknowledge the assistance of the Province of British Columbia through the British Columbia Arts Council.

Edited by Lynn Henry
Text design by Val Speidel
Cover design by Linda Gustafson / Counterpunch
Cover photograph by Gary Powell / Photonica
Author photograph by Glenn Hunter

NATIONAL LIBRARY OF CANADA CATALOGUING IN PUBLICATION DATA

Hunter, Aislinn, 1969–
  What's left us

  ISBN 1-55192-412-9

  I. Title.
PS8565.US766W52 2001   C813'.6   C2001-910225-9
PR9199.3.H824W52 2001

Polestar, an Imprint of Raincoast Books
9050 Shaughnessy Street
Vancouver, British Columbia
Canada   V6P 6E5
www.raincoast.com

1 2 3 4 5 6 7 8 9 10

Printed and bound in Canada.

LITERATURE AND LANGUAGE DIVISION
LITERATURE INFORMATION CENTER
THE CHICAGO PUBLIC LIBRARY
400 SOUTH STATE STREET
CHICAGO, ILLINOIS 60605

For my mother

Contents

THE STORIES

THE NOVELLA

"To dare to be born.
To bare love."

— Elizabeth Smart, *The Assumption of Rogues and Rascals*

THE STORIES

Hagiography

SOPHIE BELIEVED SHE HAD been called by the Divine to work at the Ormand Quay Triple X Cinema. First of all, she was good with numbers.

"Four pounds a ticket, times two shows, equals eight pounds. Add popcorn" (stale and overly salted) "at fifty-five pence—equals eight pounds fifty-five pence total."

She smiled brightly and put the gentleman's money in the old tin cash box.

"Next?"

Second, she was a devout and God-fearing Catholic girl who at twenty-one was at her peak of sexual repression. Divinity, Sophie and her mother decided, had called her to test herself. Besides, the only other places that were hiring in all of Dublin were the pubs, and Sophie's mother didn't care for the drink at all.

Sophie liked candy-apple red lip colour and short skirts that swirled around her ordinary thighs as she walked down O'Connell Street to work. She had learned to think of herself as plain and had given up all hope of ever being beautiful. It was, she reasoned, her individual features that never quite seemed pulled together. Often she caught sight of her reflection in shop windows: nose too long for her face, lipstick on her teeth, frizzy brown hair popping out of her barrettes. Behind the Plexiglas in the ticket booth, however, she felt desirable. She ignored the water stains marking the peeled yellow wallpaper and the cigarette burns along the counter. She sat up straight and focused on the task at hand.

The flicks at the Triple X ran at nine and eleven. There was always a fair enough crowd, especially for the American imports. "The Irish like nothing better," Peter the projectionist liked to remark, "than American smut. Reminds us of our blessed sanctity." He said this every time an American film was showing, chuckling more to himself than to anyone else. Sophie knew the Western pornos were Peter's favourites, better than the British films they usually showed. The American films were said to be the most outrageous. Films like *Way Down South* and *Cowboy Riders* were considered classics.

"Four pounds please," Sophie says to the next man in the queue. Tonight she is feeling kind of pretty in her mother's light blue summer dress and knitted shawl. She leans towards the cut oval in the Plexiglas, slipping her hand underneath it to take the fellow's fiver. "Grand," she smiles widely, "one pound's yer change." She gives him back his coin, lets her fingers rest on his hand momentarily.

This is not about him. There are many men, mostly in their forties, whose hands Sophie brushes from the comfort of her red vinyl stool. This is not about numbers, unless numerology dictates fate and every cash transaction in the ticket booth or in Dublin leads to it. This is not about sex, although eventually we'll get to that. There is a young seminarian at Saint Patrick's College. His name is James, after the biblical James; we are, after all, in Ireland. Young James loves God, also feels compelled by

Grace, Divinity, his ma, what have you, to his vocation. The Lord, he believes, is his shepherd, there is nothing he should want. He will come to want Sophie.

James first meets Sophie on an April day, halfway down Grafton Street. He's bent over the cobblestones, tapping his finger on the ground.

"All right there?"

First he sees her ankles, sloppy flats, and then his head follows his eyes up her bare and goose-pimpled leg to her thick waist, round breasts and finally her face. It's pinched.

"All right or not? Are you daft?"

People pass by them. James clears his throat, shifts so Sophie's blocking the sun again.

"Sorry?"

"Did you lose something?"

He looks at the cobblestones in front of where he's kneeling.

"Ah, no."

Sophie, puckering her lips, surveys the street. People come and go from shops and offices.

"So?" she folds her arms." Do you need a hand or not?"

"Something's written here," he says.

"Oh." She leans over and her blouse and cardigan open a bit. Sure enough there are illegible scribbles over three of the stones.

"I can't read it," he sighs.

Standing up next to her James feels tall and lanky. His dark fringe flops in front of his eyes and he brushes it aside impatiently. Sophie looks at him for a moment as if he is familiar, but not quite.

"All right," she sighs, "good enough then." And she strides away.

Hagiography

James and Sophie both love God. And they both love their respective parents who love God more than Sophie and James ever could. Both families share a number of traditions: confession and communion, charity work with those less fortunate, and the quiet kind of self-flagellation that comes from wondering if you love God enough. James is ready to give himself to God. But something about Sophie has bowled him over. There is, in truth, a lot of love going around—mostly, but not entirely, of the holy kind.

Later that week Sophie locks the ticket booth and sneaks up to the projection room for the first time in the seven months she's worked at the Triple X. She can't quite put her finger on it but she's feeling a little unsettled. Maybe, she reasons, it was not being able to read that scrawl on the stones on Grafton Street. As if she's missing a sign.

Two light knocks on the projection room door get no response so Sophie lets herself in. Peter's mangy head is pressed close to the projector and he's looking through the hole around the lens. He's got his hand around his penis, which surprises Sophie because she'd never really considered the possibility of it before. Averting her eyes, she takes in the nudie pin-ups tacked over the wood panelling.

"Humph." She clears her throat loudly. "Peter?"

"Yeah?" He barely turns towards her.

She's curious about the film but doesn't want to actually look at it. That, she figures, would be a sin.

"What?" He's impatient.

"Is it any good?"

James is good. Clean undies every day, never curses, respects his mother, does up the dishes after dinner, helps old ladies and so on. He makes the long trek from his flat in Parnell Square to Saint Patrick's College in Maynooth every day. He speaks both Irish and Latin. Coming home he recites the Bible under his breath, crossing in front of the pawnshops and military surplus stores that blanket Capel Street. He has memorized Genesis and the Revelations, the Psalms, Matthew and Mark. Today, a Sunday, he peers through the window of a sun-filled bakery and, seeing the scones, decides to indulge.

"Two please."

"One pound sixty."

Through the shop window, between shelves loaded with sourdough and rye, he spies Sophie.

"Keep it," he says and leaves without his change, without his scones.

She would be perfect, he thinks, his pace quickening to catch up to Sophie, perfect on a carousel, sitting sidesaddle on a creamy palomino, her halo of hair catching the sunlight, her arm swinging open to him as she kicks off her loafers. She would be perfect if he could place her there in real life, at the carnival that came to Bray every summer when he was growing up. It was the most complete part of his childhood, the most freedom he'd ever felt. Flickering lights strung up like stars from Bray Head to the causeway and dozens of rides, side shows. Going round on the carousel, you could sometimes get a glimpse into the fat lady's tent, catch sight of her large drooping breasts before the tent flap closed behind another customer. At the carnival, whole worlds that James had never considered were revealed. On top of the ferris wheel, James, only twelve, looked down at the smallness of the people below. He raised his arms to the sky, knowing

Hagiography

there was nothing left between him and heaven. It was then, on that ferris wheel, that James first knew God.

At Ha'penny Bridge he is almost beside her. Unsure if he should actually touch this woman, he simply lopes along at a distance, thinking of ferris wheels and cotton candy, the pink of her cardigan. The more he muses the more he wants to touch her.

"Ms.—" His hand—long, clean fingers—reaches out to her shoulder as she turns onto the sidewalk, but she picks up her pace before he can reach her. Sophie, oblivious to James' presence, looks both ways then trots across the street and enters a narrow utility doorway. "No Entrance" is written boldly above the door handle in black spray paint. Above his head to the left James sees the marquee.

Triple X.

Water Orgy and *All Wet*. Double bill.

Flummoxed, James takes a step back, rereads the sign. He decides he'll wait.

These are the options that are open to him: James can leave and pretend he didn't see Sophie. He can retrace his steps, go back to the bakery and then enter in under the ringing bells above the door. Embarrassed, he can ask the counter girl if she remembers him, and if so, could he still take the scones. Or, James could go in through the No Entrance doorway and seek out Sophie. He could put his hand out to her and bring her out of the Triple X and into the bright cast of the day. But it is a foreboding door and the fear of being seen stops him.

"Peter?" Sophie sees the projectionist down the faintly lit hallway.

"Over here darlin'."

"Cheques?"

"Sam's got 'em." He jabs his thumb towards the office.

Sophie moves to squeeze by Peter, who is reclining against the wall outside the office doorway. He takes a deep drag of his cigarette then flicks the ashes over the carpet, running his hand up Sophie's leg when she makes her way past him.

"Really?" she smiles, jabs him hard with her knuckle.

"All's fair," he mumbles, "all's fair."

Outside, Sophie hustles towards home, opening her envelope to check her wage card. James is following her. She adds up the figures in her head, mumbles little bits, "times eight ..., for taxes." Stuffing the envelope into her handbag, Sophie misses the light and steps out off the curb. It is mid-morning now and the traffic is thin. Nonetheless a lorry is barreling towards her and, of course, the driver has his mind on other things.

The predicament is this: Sophie is still oblivious to her calling. James, however, is not. He loves Sophie more than he loves God and they've only just met. The lorry is barreling down.

The lorry is barreling down. The lorry driver has six children and a wife who cross-stitches and embroiders beautifully. It is not a happy home, but it is typical, and "typical" is well-documented and quite routine in this country. Sophie steps out, typically. The driver has just noticed a spot on his trousers and is looking at it, wondering how it got there and if his wife can get it out.

Sophie steps off the curb.

James, as we have noted, is a bit too far behind.

There is the sound of brakes, there is a fantastic pause, there is a "No!" from the depths of James' soul, which is quite deep.

Hagiography

"No!" again. The lorry driver swerves. Sophie is pulled off the road by a strong ruddy hand. It is not James' hand.

Sophie marries Eamon, who is a friend of the fellow who saves her life, the fellow with the strong ruddy hand. They date for two years and have sex on their wedding night and once a week after. It is blasé at the best of times. Sophie leaves her job, foregoing her calling, her Plexiglas shrine. She is no longer a virgin, so the temptation, the test the Triple X represents, no longer seems necessary. She starts going to the pubs, although her mother threatens to disown her. In her spare time Sophie gives cooking classes at the local Catholic Woman's Association.

On a Tuesday, some four years into their marriage, Eamon is at the garage working late. That night Sophie is at home rifling through donations for the CWA's annual book sale. She happens upon a story in an American fashion magazine in which the heroine is bedded by a Montana plains man. Sophie discovers masturbation. Her happiness lasts close to six months.

But this is not about Sophie and Eamon. This is about James. Let's say the man with the ruddy hand was preoccupied, thinking about his pal Eamon who owns a garage.

The man with the ruddy hand is preoccupied, thinking about his pal Eamon who owns a garage. Eamon is fixing the ruddy-handed man's Austin. Thinking about where the money will come from, the man with the ruddy hand scuffs his toe on the pavement while he waits for the light to change. The lorry driver is looking at his pants.

Sophie steps out.

A "No!" rips through the skies and meets with the small

slender hand of one James MacNeill as he pulls on the shoulder of a woman in a pink cardigan. He loves her, but he doesn't even know her name.

Over scones with jam and tea at Bewley's (coming to a perfect four pound total), the conversation centres around not the almost accident, not numerology or *Water Orgy* but on having a calling. Sophie leans forward across the table, still exhilarated by the "No!," the rush of attention, this lanky man folding her into his arms right there on O'Connell Street. Sophie sees Divinity in James, not just in his love of God, in his thin, white seminarian collar, but in his adoration of her, in the "No!" from the depths of his soul. Sophie is leaning across the table, her blouse and cardigan opening slightly. Her feet are grazing the floor and she's watching James watch her, suddenly aware of her own beauty, even in this brightly lit café. Settling back into her chair, Sophie thinks about how perfectly it fits her body, how throne-like it is, this dark wood chair on the James Joyce floor of Bewley's Café. She reaches her hand across the table to James. She is not giving him popcorn or change. It is an offering.

James the seminarian beams up at Sophie; she is breathtaking. He is nervous because he has never wanted anything this much in his life. With his finger he traces the water mark his tea cup has left. Round and round that finger goes, like a lazy sideways ferris wheel. James notices it becoming, in its roundness, the eye of God. God is watching them, as we all are, the two of them finally together, there, in Bewley's Café. Her hand stretches out farther towards his, the offering. His hand sliding across the table to hers, fingers touching first, then palms. His sleeve blurring the water mark, the ferris wheel, the all-knowing, all-seeing eye.

We Live in this World

THE RAIN IS STREELING down my face and I can't see anything. I'm standing in the middle of the road in front of a stopped mini-van, I'm acting like a crazy person, a crazy person in dinner party clothes with a Jetta back home in her driveway and keys in her hand. The woman in the driver's seat, the woman whose eyes my eyes are meeting, stares at me past the quick swipes of her windshield wipers. In the glare of her headlights I flap my arms, I do an atrocious imitation of semaphore. When I approach her window she puts her mini van in reverse. For a few seconds I walk beside the van, gesturing for her to roll down the window. But she doesn't; instead she turns the steering wheel and goes over onto the other side of the road. She hits the accelerator and pulls away.

"I ran into Evan on the corner of 28th and Dunbar." An hour earlier, I was telling this to a table of four guests. I was telling it while they picked at their potatoes and roast.

"It was either that or the lamppost and he was the more pliable bet."

I ran into Evan.

At dinner parties I like to tell the story of how Evan and I met. It makes him uncomfortable but I still think it's a good laugh. When I tell it really well Evan laughs too, although once, about a year ago, he said he wanted to crawl under the kitchen table, pry the Viennese tile off the concrete, chip his way through the cement with his butter knife and burrow himself as far as he could underground. When I apologized that night in bed, holding his warm, still hand, begging his forgiveness, he said, "Arla, honey, it's a good story, but it's all in the telling." Meeting Evan changed me.

My mother met my father when she was nineteen. Years later she said she found it amusing, the irony of marrying a podiatrist whose greatest disappointment in life would be that his only daughter inherited her mother's wonky feet. This from a man who'd fathered a delusional son, who'd jumped ship before things got really crazy.

My first memory of my father is as follows: I'm twirling around in the basement of our house in Sudbury, I'm four years old, doing semi-cartwheels, clumsy pirouettes on the brown carpet, wiping out after a half-turn, grazing my knees on the shag. I get up, looking over at him in the wingback chair to see if he's still watching. He is, so I make a great Y of my arms like a magician's assistant, and tumble over onto the flats of my palms. I scissor for a second in midair, holding a precarious balance. Back on my feet I say, "Look Daddy, look Daddy, look Daddy, look." I make a song out of it, I jump and twirl, I try to do it again. He claps, claps loud, but when the whole production is finished, he takes me up onto his lap, says, "Sweetie, you'll never be a dancer with those feet."

My brother will never be anything. He can barely hold down a job. In fact, my brother is nuts. At least, that's what I say when no one else is around and I don't care about being politically correct. Other times I refer to him as The Wanker. With my mom I simply call him Jeb. And he isn't nuts anyway, that's entirely incorrect unless you call running down the street in your underwear nuts, unless you call breaking into your sister's art gallery super-crazy-mad out of control. Every other Wednesday, we used to go to the grotty little group home where Jeb lives, Evan and I, but only because my mother insisted we go. But it wasn't fair to Evan at all. Sometimes he has a hard enough time because he feels hedged-in by our lily-of-the-valley walls, by our bright-as-floodlight windows.

During tonight's dinner party our dog Rupert, our instrument of good fortune, ambled into the dining room as if on cue. In reality he was just smelling the gravy, had probably heard the forks scraping the last remnants of roast off the plates. Geena, a painter from Victoria who'd never been to the house before, looked at Rupert like he was something out of the Brothers Grimm, like he was a black bear who'd wandered into the dining room in search of berries. He noticed that and went to stand beside her, wagging his tail like a metronome against the side of her chair while I went on with my story.

"Rupert had taken off at 27th with me flailing along behind him."

Flailing along as if his leash was some kind of umbilicus, as if I was incapable of letting go.

"And then BAM, I plowed right into Evan."

Geena smiled at that. Bowled over by love she might have been thinking. And that's what I was thinking too. With a little encouragement I launched into the details—how Rupert relieved himself on the Canadian Imperial Bank of Commerce wall, how I practically had to haul Evan to his feet, how he was shaking so much I thought I'd have to fireman-carry him home. Everyone laughed at that, except Ellen. She just smiled a little, her fingers moving slowly over the curve of her throat.

I went on. I told our dinner guests how once up off the ground, Evan looked at me with his jaw hanging open, how his breathing had gone all weird. I told them that he reminded me of one of those public service commercials featuring the good-looking guy who's just a bit odd. The kind of guy you think you could fall for before the voice-over says something like "One out of every five Canadians has a mental disorder."

Jordie, Geena and Bryce laughed. Evan smiled at me across the table, then he pushed back his chair as if to signal that he was a minute away from starting to degrout the tile. Ellen pushed a dark strand of hair away from her face. I saw Evan watch her hand, pale and swan-like, returning to her lap. He excused himself and went into the kitchen.

"Anyway," I said cheerfully, "right off the bat I was smitten."

My parents met through one of my mother's friends. It was a blind date, which I suppose is its own kind of accident. My father was already in med school and he had a car, a baby blue Chevy Bel Air. On their first date my father drove my mother from Sudbury to Niagara Falls because she said she'd never been there. It was a romantic gesture that didn't quite pan out. They spent six hours on the road dodging highway construction, the A.M. radio on and neither of them knowing the same songs. Dad once described how Mom had her hair up, how every time he turned towards her the sunlight was shining on her hairpins. He used to say with a wink, "I thought your mother was sparkling."

My mother always had the best intentions. She always tried to make things work. I remember when Jeb was ten he wanted to join the U.S. Marines, a by-product of the three years our family lived in Windsor, Ontario, three years in which Jeb was glued to American television. My mother thought the hours spent in front of the TV explained Jeb's outbursts: he needed to get out more, she said, and so logically she took him to the Checker Flag Raceway, to wrestling matches at Cobo Arena, to rodeos out in Essex County. She presented him with what she thought were constructive uses of testosterone. He had, after all, been kidnapping the neighbour's cat, he'd been throwing rocks through the school windows.

Over the years my mother acquired a number of books advising parents how to deal with difficult children. And to her credit she is both inventive and flexible. My mother is capable of adapting the warm fuzzy/cold prickly parenting theory that worked in 1972 into something a little more radical for the year 2001. Now she calls it affirmation/confrontation: "You are my son, Jeb, and I love you but I don't always like the things you do."

I will confess that my mother is versatile, I will admit she is extremely capable, but I can't say she did really well with me. If I'd had the kind of parenting a child in a reasonable family might have been granted I wouldn't be standing in a strapless dress in the pouring rain trying to find a taxi. I wouldn't be trying to flag down strangers. For a second I imagine that this must be what Jeb feels like, that I've finally arrived at loopy, lost-it, out-of-control. Two more cars go by on Dunbar so I start heading towards the shops to find a phone. I start to hiccup and then I start crying. I get a glimpse of myself in the window of a parked car and I fancy that I look a bit like Sylvia Plath. This gets me laughing but it also illustrates my point. If my mother had done better by me I might be able to deal with a crisis, I might be able to handle myself with some measure of aplomb.

Most days when I look at my mother I see Betty Crocker. Betty Crocker hiding under the guise of a Martha Stewart blunt cut with Martha Stewart honey-blonde highlights. Although, that said, up until five years ago she looked very Jackie Swann. Her lapels, when she wore them, were four inches too wide. I remember taking her to Marks and Spencer one year on her birthday. I pulled a wool jacket off the spin-rack of new fall clothes and held it out for her. She said, "Arla, I don't have money to throw around on a new blazer." I could have told her it was intended as a gift; instead, all I said was, "It's a suit jacket." Ours has always been a relationship of semantics.

My mother is a secretary in a secretarial pool, which when you say it, evokes an image of Esther Williams. Sometimes I've imagined her and her co-workers sitting at their desks in rubber swim caps, wearing nose clips. I imagine for sport they practice synco-typing, flipping their feet around under the desks as if they're in a wading pool.

Evan eventually came back from the kitchen. He started clearing the dinner plates. Bryce, Ellen's boyfriend, hadn't touched the roast. He's probably one of those polite vegetarians who doesn't complain, who quietly picks at anything that escapes the ladle of gravy. When Evan sat down, Ellen, who's a sculptor, said, "Arla's still describing the events that led up to your engagement." I looked over at Evan and he looked away. Then Rupert went over to him, leaned up against his chair. The dog always does that when he's picking sides. When I started into the story again Rupert plunked his big black head down on Evan's lap, his wolfish eyes watching me.

"So we went for coffee at Carlotto's," I told them, "and Evan was still shaking. Then he sat down and said it. Just like that and as soon as the word was out of his mouth he became placid. I mean, calm as a lake. 'I'm agoraphobic,' he said, then this—I don't know—serenity just washed over him. Meanwhile, I was thinking angora-phobic? Fear of fuzzy sweaters? I mean I was all of twenty-four, I just didn't know."

In the kitchen the phone rang. A look of relief, a saved-by-the-bell, thank-God-people-still-call-during-the-dinner-hour expression, came over Evan's face. I excused myself and walked around the corner to the phone. I picked up the receiver.

"Hello?" and for a few seconds there was nothing. "Hello?" I said again, peeking around the corner and into the dining room. Evan was saying something and Geena and Ellen were laughing.

"Arla?" It was mom. Her voice was cracking. A minute later I was out the front door and running down the road.

My mother likes sermons. She always ensures I'm sitting down before delivering one. This should have ended when I turned thirty, but it seems to go on and on. For example, a few weeks ago I was over at the house to help her put up new shelves in the laundry room. "Come here," she said and dragged me into the kitchen. Right away I saw it coming. I always see it coming, it's like those last few minutes before a tornado, the room gets very still and quiet, everything turns a bit green. My mother's advice always comes when she's wearing oven mitts. This is no joke. Huge, blue, quilted oven mitts covered in mosquito-sized yellow flowers. The mitts go on and, boom, she seems to have something to say, something like, "Listen, I think you should see Jeb more often. He is your brother, you know."

Once when she went out of the kitchen leaving the gloves hanging over the oven rail, leaving them there like dejected puppets, I looked inside the grey nubby interiors to see what could possibly possess her to deliver her sermons only when they'd been donned. Nothing. Only a few crumbs knit into the cotton, only burled bits of grey pill, the quashed indent of her hand.

I was eleven the first time my father went to Florida for part of the winter. He liked to golf and a few of his friends had gone down there in semi-retirement. Two days after he left, Jeb managed to get arrested. He'd kicked down the neighbour's picket fence, breaking half the boards over his knee. All told, it took him two hours to do it.

Once Jeb was under control, my mother called my dad at the bungalow in Florida and relayed the tale while I made us dinner. I remember her asking Dad to come home, I remember her slapping a dishtowel against the back of the kitchen chair, trying to contain her exasperation. Two weeks later when my dad came back, we packed up and moved from Ontario to Vancouver. Jeb went into a kids-like-Jeb kind of school.

The year I decided to become an artist was the year Jeb really lost it, it was the year Dad moved down to Florida for good. I'd given Dad my first painting as a going away gift and, happy with it, he'd said, "You may have inherited your mother's duck feet but at least you have my hands." Later that summer I brought home a watercolour of the Burrard Street Bridge and my mother, on the phone with Jeb's counsellor, had nodded as a way of appraising it. Ten minutes later we were down on Hastings in her Cavalier, the Burrard Street Bridge spanning the backseat in all its pastel glory while we tried to track down Jeb. The counsellor had called to say she thought he was messing around with his drugs again. "How can she tell?" I'd snapped. "He only has a seven-pill-a-day regimen."

We found him sitting on the corner near Main. "My God," I remember my mother saying, getting out of the driver's seat, "he looks so thin."

I finally manage to hail a cab on Dunbar. I feel like I've been walking around out here for an hour, the rain like bullets, my dress something of a second skin. It could only pour like this in Vancouver. My father always said things like that, he liked to comment on the weather as if he'd forged a profession out of studying Pacific-style monsoons. My father the podiatrist/meteorologist, my father who, if he were here, would be like Gene Kelly, tap tapping and humming, ignoring the situation with Jeb, mulling over the effect of El Niño in this fucking unnatural rain. I've lost one of my shoes. Down the street I hear Evan calling me.

I remember bringing Evan home that first evening. I know this sounds like the kind of thing a person might say about a stray dog or cat, but, truth be told, there was an element of rescue in it. But that's something I keep between us, that isn't dinner party conversation. First we had coffee, then we walked around the Dunbar Community Centre talking, looping the brick building again and again as if we were in orbit. I remember the tree branches doing callisthenics overhead, Rupert dragging his leash through piles of leaves. I remember Evan asking me a hundred questions about my art. I slept with Evan that night. But first we went back to his basement suite under his parents' house. He must have known where things were headed because I remember him going into the bathroom, brushing his teeth.

It was saying the word "agoraphobic" that made Evan seem

more relaxed. After making our way around the Community Centre he became an animated person whose only odd attribute was hesitancy. If there was a hurdle he'd bounded over it like an athlete and so, some seven hours later, there we were, sitting on the lawn outside my house, the sky going dark around us. Evan was pulling at the long blades of grass, twisting their stems with his fingers. He was telling me how long it had taken him to get to the point where he could walk down the street without losing it. A gust of wind tossed a handful of acorns down from the tree just as he said that, and Evan didn't even flinch.

I know exactly how many times my mother and I had to go for Jeb after that first incident. Twenty-seven. And then there was the time he was in the police station, when they caught him breaking into the art gallery where I worked. He'd flung a rock through the window.

I smiled at the lieutenant when we picked up Jeb, I shrugged it all off, I said, "At least my brother's procured an interest in art."

Twenty-seven times. It would go like this:

"Get in the car."

"Fuck off."

"Jeb!"

"Call me Andy." Neither of us particularly liked our Beverly Hillbilly names.

"OK. Andy. Andy please get in the car. Come on."

And we'd be driving down Hastings at a snail's pace, my mother and I, trying to convince him to get in the car, the line-up of traffic behind us honking.

More often than not, Jeb got in. He'd go back to the doctors and the group home and they'd try again to adjust his meds or they'd throw him in another group home where the people were just as fucked-up and luckless and they'd call it rehab instead of monitored living. Once when I went all the way in, when I walked him back up to his room, I noticed there were straps on the side bars of the bed. My brother like someone in the loony bin, like Harry Houdini without the tricks.

My mother acts pleased through clenched teeth. I was twenty-three when I first saw it. I brought her unacceptable boyfriends, I brought her a blouse stained with salad oil, I brought her over-due taxes and complaints around issues like water retention. I visited wearing sporty well-heeled sandals and a skirt with no slip, all the signs that her daughter was too liberal and probably having regular sex. I brought her a painting of a giant green swirling vagina. She said, "Nice forest, Honey, very Emily Carr." She said, "We have to visit Jeb today, they're switching his meds."

I held up the painting so she'd really look at it, I held it up and she squinted. Moving closer she said, "Pines or cedar?"

I told her I'd titled it "Orgasm," and she stepped back a bit, tilted her head, said, "I had no idea you felt that way about the forest."

Evan's gripe has always been with the word. Well, not even the word. After we'd been dating a while we were sitting out in the back yard surrounded by the thick wall of holly bushes his parents had transplanted for him. Their yard always struck me as something of a cheerful prison, with its plank wood fence, tall bushes and rhododendrons galore.

He said, "Consider the word."

I mulled it over.

"First of all, people can't say it."

I tried. I was relaxed, the sun was out, the skies were blue and even though a particularly hostile honeybee was taking great delight in blasting around my left ear, I remember feeling happy, I remember wanting to please him.

"Agor-a-phobic." I said it, I shrugged.

He smiled. Touched my lip with his finger. No, marveled at my lip while touching it with his finger. I remember thinking how easy it must be to be in love when you've never even had a girlfriend.

"It means fear of the marketplace," he said. "Fear of assembly."

I crossed and uncrossed my legs, made scissor motions over the bristle of the grass. I felt like a kid again.

Rupert came up to us then and nuzzled Evan's face. Evan said, "I'm not very fond of dogs, you know." But Rupert stood there oblivious, his mouth open and his tongue slung out the side. "Come here, Rupe." I called the dog over to me but he wouldn't come. I looked over at Evan apologetically. There were times I could still catch him shaking.

A few weeks after I met Evan I called my mother. "I'm coming over," I said. I said it with the kind of urgency someone would only expect from Jeb. I wanted to tell her about Evan. That I'd met the man I wanted to marry. She slipped on the oven mitts two minutes after I was in the door. I told her I met an agoraphobic man on the street. She pretended she didn't hear me.

"I met an agoraphobic man," I said. "I literally ran into him and now we're dating."

Her selective hearing has always been like a radio that's just missing its station.

She said, "But Arla, it isn't really the time of the year to start raking."

Years ago I started compiling a list of things that I know my mother must have heard me say, things she might be saving for later conversations: I have sold a number of paintings; I always thought Dad would come back; I'm thinking of getting a tattoo; I'm thinking of moving to Toronto. After leaving the house that afternoon I added: I met an agoraphobic man and I slept with him as a way of saying hello.

Two weeks after our family had packed up and moved to Vancouver, Jeb started at the school for undiagnosed-loony-tunes. He was fourteen. I remember the panicked look on his face as he stood at the bottom of the steps waiting for the bus. I remember that my mom and I went and stood on the sidewalk with him.

Like Evan, Jeb also has problems with the word. He doesn't like to be called crazy, he prefers "fucked-up." These days the *Diagnostic and Statistical Manual* calls it "borderline personality disorder." Borderline personality disorder. I think it sounds like a busy tourist outlet in a wayside Southern town. I think it sounds like something you can step out of.

The taxi driver sees me shaking and he cranks up the heat. My hands are trembling so much in my lap that I decide to sit on them. The windshield wipers are working at rain that's falling in sheets, the wipers doing nothing but delineating waves. The driver looks at me in his rearview mirror as we peel away from a red light. He knows better than to say anything. Mom will be there by now. We're meeting at the hospital.

Evan changed me. It wasn't the other way around. His therapist credits me with how quickly he got better but he was already well on his way. I like to tell the story of how we met because in truth I think Evan found me. I tell it so people will know how lucky I think I am. Later I'll call him from a pay phone, I'll say I'm sorry I ran out, I'll tell him I wasn't thinking, I'll ask if the guests got home okay. I'll inquire about Ellen, I'll call her Anna Pavlova, which always makes him laugh. "Ellen the swan," I'll say, "Ellen the goose, Ellen the quacker." And Evan will laugh, he'll say, "Arla, most people don't talk about their best friend that way."

My mother and I stand beside the bed and listen to the woman humming on the other side of the curtain. The smell of antiseptic tickles my nose, burns the back of my throat. My mother is looking at Jeb, mumbling, "He's so thin," as if the one thing she wanted to do in life was feed him. My brother is there, on the bed, tubes running in and out of him, he is there with matted hair and a new sickle-shaped scar on his chin, a row of bruises on his upper arm like a trail of violets. This is my brother two hours after they found him in his room at the halfway house, this is my brother in the absolute peace of a drug-induced coma. This is my brother who will never come clean.

My mother and I walk across the street to Denny's. We go and we sit under the brightest fluorescent lighting I've ever come across in my life. I decide it's the kind of lighting they use to illuminate photo sessions, sessions that produce the kind of glossy food images we find illustrated on the Denny's menu cover. In fact, when the food arrives it bears a glistening and exact resemblance to the images we have perused while ordering. I say, "My burger is glaring," and my mother ignores me, sips on her Coke.

There are things we don't talk about. Sex is one. What happened between her and my father is another. We don't talk about how I think Evan and Ellen are having an affair, how the very rhyme of their names annoys me. Instead we talk about the cut on Jeb's chin, then we wonder to ourselves how he got it.

My mother once told me that during a fight my father put his fist through the headboard of their bed. She said I didn't know what kind of man he could be. She said that I only remembered piggyback rides and dance lessons, how he drove me downtown to my ballet class twice a week while she stayed home with Jeb. That kind of revelation is a rare occurrence in our family, like a window finally open, the weight of the drapes only apparent when they're gone.

We sit in Denny's and I try to make a straight line out of the past two hours, try to organize what the doctor, the specialist and the nurse said. I try to plot it out, put it in order: the phone call, the dinner, standing on the road for what felt like years. Somewhere along the way I lost my shoes. I show my mother, poke my foot out from under the table: shredded nylons, pale skin, the blue trail of veins. My mother pokes her foot out too and I realize she's still in her slippers. She smiles at how ridiculous we must seem and I blow air bubbles down the straw of my Coke because I'm laughing.

Jeb is in a coma, huddling in the warm cocoon of his quietly ticking brain. And my mother and I are suddenly without him. It's as if he's turned a corner, as if he's gone out the front door and down the walkway. It's as if he didn't look back, as if he kept going. My mother and I under the too-bright fluorescent lights of Denny's ask how each other's meal was, ask out of courtesy as if we're sitting together for the first time. Like my mother and father in the car driving to Niagara Falls on their first date, the windows open as they head past Lake Huron, the pins in her hair shining and all the possibilities of what they might say laid out like the rutted road ahead.

We Live in this World

Unto Herself

LOVE, SHE DECIDED, was a windy country, a two-storey stucco in the path of disaster, a glued together door frame, a loose hinge. Love was a continual state of disrepair and ironically she'd married the carpenter.

"She" is a cozy bed-sit, stacked washer-dryer, kitchen built into the wall without much room for manoeuvring. She is a woman worn down, waiting at six P.M. on a Friday for her husband to come home for his lacklustre dinner. Marriage had marked the end of Nora's mobility, the loss of high ceilings, not to mention her culinary skills. Well, after that first week at any rate, when Salmon in Raspberry Cream Sauce and Spinach Ricotta Soufflé went unappreciated, then made the rounds as a point of humour with the lads down at the pub. "Nora the cook," they called her, "the haute cuisine housewife."

They made her small, but "she" used to be a flat unto herself. Modest three rooms with a coin-box shower, a window that opened onto the back deck over a garden in the hub of Rathmines. The room arrangements, she knew, were simple, the furniture worn, but it was what she had salvaged from her parents' attic, and it was hers. The only investment had been her bed, which was, in fact, too narrow, the thick blue down duvet decadent enough to make up for all that was average. Nora could always make the best of everything, add her little touches, a vase of fresh daisies, throw pillows, the odd cluster of framed photographs on the monotone walls. It was while living here that she'd found the carpenter half-lit in the entry hallway, straddling the front door and tooling with the lock mechanism. "Been broke fer a month," she'd said as she stepped over him onto the walkway. "Mind yourself," he'd muttered, almost into the bell of her skirt.

Whatever "he" had been before they met, it must have been large and spacious, like his hands. In ownership, probably his parents' because, even after the engagement, he never took her there. It must, she reasoned, have had a workshop out back where he'd spent his days caught up in the loud whirl of the power saw, the air thick with motes of dust. He was never, in her estimation, a people person. He liked enclosed spaces, doors with latches.

At present, however, he is absent, a garage without a garage door, just three walls encompassing a Vauxhall with shite for brakes, a car with cables that might snap any day and start the slow roll down the driveway into the neighbours' begonias or over their saggy-bellied calico cat. And so, on this, an unspectacular evening in August, Nora fiddles around the house polishing already shiny silver, thinking about the imminent automotive disaster and her husband, who is undoubtedly a square concrete room housing a beat-up auto and a dozen boxes marked "For the Rummage Sale." "He" is this, at the absolute best. For months there's been nothing between them save her requests for conversation and his outbursts over breakfast when the look of her snivelling over her sunny-side ups was more than he could, apparently, bear.

"They" are 1 Bainsbridge Road, this is their fixed address, and certainly the decor is modern, the corners free of cobwebs, the company often bland or innocuous enough. "She" may have been whittled down to a bed-sit but in truth she has never lived so spaciously, never had carpets so lush, never had such a banister and stairs to descend from. Everything was in perfect order except for the doors. First the garage, unfailingly open, and now, as if his quiet excursions out the back door weren't enough, it's the front entry come ajar. A solid-looking wood door painted yellow, a "1" fixed firmly in brass where a window might have been cut, seemingly stable enough, but now the frame's splitting slightly at the seams and the hinge with the cockeyed screw is nearly undone again. When they met he was fixing the door in Rathmines; he has fixed a hundred doors since, including this one. Last week, however, he threw his hands up in the air, tugged at his shirt collar and left it askew. "Nothing to be done," he'd said, as if the whole house was irreparably damaged, as if a violent wind storm had levelled the whole of Dublin. "It's only a hinge," she replied, but he was already out the door, toolbox in hand, off to fix entries in other houses, in other parts of the city.

"And so?" she asks herself, ignoring the dinner she laid out, wiping the counter again. A rust stain from last week's stew can is still fixed on the blue arborite, regardless of attempts to remove it with cleanser. Nora turns towards the entry hall, dishcloth in hand, and because it must be done, resolves to give the door a go herself. She digs through the odd sods in his tool cabinet and finds only sandpaper, saw blades, ratchets and bits. Behind the empty paint cans she finds his favourite tape measure, a broken pencil, some mothballs. The screwdriver and the carpenter's glue must be with him. And where, then, is the carpenter? The carpenter. Nora's mind runs round the question and she comes back to architecture, blank spaces framed by immense rafters, two rows of people cheering them up the aisle. "God bless, Nora, God bless," and only her mother scowling at her daughter's fourth month of pregnancy hidden under the empire waistline of her wedding dress. "God bless," right up to the day they moved into Bainsbridge, the cardboard box of sewing and needlepoint falling to her feet with something else, which did a slow waterdance down. The end of it confirmed by ultrasound and now only blank spaces.

Still at a loss for tools, for the carpenter, for everything, Nora runs her hands along the upper metal shelves of his tool cabinet. Nothing. As empty as the trip up the stairwell, the view from the front door down Leinster Road. No one to be seen at six in the evening when all good folk are in their homes eating their roast and potatoes. No one to be seen at all. Roast here on the table and overcooked at that, but no matter as there is something else still askew. The door. The door, and the carpenter. The roast should have been taken out of the oven before six. Her fault entirely. And the carpenter, Nora finally acknowledges, has run off with the lingerie salesgirl from Stephen's Green Centre. A wee blonde who had a laminated tag on her blouse pocket, some flower or another for a name. Daisy, was it? No. Petunia? Rose? Ah, Lily. He's run off with the pixie girl called Lily, for the weekend anyway, and Nora's in the house with her altogether numb body, the door askew, wind rattling the windowpanes.

She sits on her queen-size bed and surveys the light blue wallpaper that neither of them ever liked. Downstairs, the door is ajar, Nora having managed to completely unhinge it, but failing when she tried to hold it in place and put in the new screws. The wallpaper, on which she focuses, consists of small clusters of flowers in Victorian-style oval frames. Lilies, Nora fancies, although more likely some version of marigold. Nora's mind slips gears just then, and she begins to concentrate on the untoward woman called Lily. She is an American living in Ireland, undoubtedly revelling in her foreignness, her staff discounts, purple satin bustiers, silk camisoles and the like. Nothing to her beyond the changing room she cleans with Shine More every night at closing. Lily, then, is, like the carpenter, a series of attached walls. He is the garage without a door and she is the changing room propped up in the back of a gimmicky and over-priced store with its 2-for-1 signs and made-up counter girls who mutter "Oh, it's lovely on you, Ms.," or, "Sure to be a hit with the husband now," in thick Limerick accents.

That day, two Saturdays ago, Nora first saw Lily. A slight girl with her hair bundled up on her head smiling as she cracked open the door to take the medium half-slip out of Nora's hand. "Do you need a large to try as well?" the pixie asked, puckering her Really Red lips while examining them in the changing room mirror. The carpenter at the front of the store leaned over the counter. Nora disliked her before she'd even really caught on. An airiness about her, as if she was as insubstantial as a light breeze that raises the hair on the back of your neck before van-ishing entirely. That girl, obviously still in her early twenties, was as vacant as the three-by-three cubicle in which Nora stood. What was there to her anyway, save for some lingerie strewn about inside and a few tightly screwed in hooks opposite the door. "No, the medium's fine." And that was it, aside from a vague notion of excitement on the carpenter's behalf as he paid the giddy clerk who, giggling, handed him back his VISA and then carefully wrapped the half-slip which Nora, most often in her house coat, has yet to wear.

"She" would like to be a garden. Something along the lines of Phoenix Park. A wide open space, a well-treed space, a space with buildings, a space with flowers, a space with families and children picnicking on Sunday afternoons. But at twenty-nine and three-quarters she is 1 Bainsbridge Road, and on the day she moved in here, Nora became a two-bedroom house without any use for the second bedroom, the nursery already painted, the crib in place and the door quietly but firmly closed.

Abandoning their bedroom and its wallpaper, Nora heads for the nursery and opens the door. Something should happen, she thinks, but it doesn't, and so she goes right into the room, up to the crib, putting her hands on the railing. She is still not satisfied, she is still restless. There is a light film of dust, thicker along the sloping headboard. He'd wanted to get started on it early, so it would be ready in time; she remembers him saying that, as if it might take months, but he built it in an afternoon. Even made the dowels by hand. "Here it is," he'd said, taking her out onto the lawn and then pulling the tarp down inside the back of his van. A wide-eyed "ta-da!" expression on his face, probably the happiest she'd ever seen him.

Nora turns to leave the nursery but one hand is still fastened to the crib railing. She takes a step and the crib nudges forward on its wheels as if to follow her. She tugs again. The crib moves a few inches over the carpet. Pretty soon she is wedging it out of the nursery itself, scraping the white door, leaving brownish scuffs along the way. At the top of the stairs she grabs the headboard, starts down. The weight of the crib against her, she leans into it, keeps it from descending more than a few steps at a time.

Grabbing the keys off the hook by the door to the garage, she slides into the Vauxhall in her yellow housedress without her purse or her licence. She secures the crib on the roof, yanks down hard on the bungee straps that run along the interior of the roof and, deciding the tension will do, gets ready to embark.

Taking a minute to smooth her hair and push it out of her eyes before turning the ignition, Nora at the last second thinks about stepping out and peering under the car to be sure the neighbour's cat isn't napping underneath. Instead she honks the horn twice, then backs out at full speed. The crib's headboard hits the garage ceiling where it dips down over the open doorway. There's a loud crack, the bungee cords make a twanging sound, reverberate for a second, but hold.

Once out on Leinster Street Nora becomes focused, with the automated clarity of a driver whose thought processes are on standby as long as the vehicle is in motion. Stop. Signal. Advance. Turn. Accelerate. She finds herself heading down Crumlin and taking a left on Dolphin Road. On standby and, therefore, not in the frame of mind to question, she follows her hands, which turn the steering wheel left and right appropriately. She might, she briefly considers, be looking for the carpenter and, in fact, she does drive by Stephen's Green Centre. It occurs to her now that he might be there and that he might see her drive by with the Vauxhall, an oak crib strapped to the roof.

Nora circles the Green twice then gives up, turns left and once she's over Grand Canal she sees that Phoenix Park is where she's headed. Besides, she thinks, what could the carpenter do for her if found? Aside from a few nights of dancing at the Wexford, and the flowers on their first anniversary, he has been inept and preoccupied from the beginning. He'd be more interested in the broken headboard than in her state of mind. He's only a carpenter. Even with doors he just tightens screws until they let loose again, and what's the use in that?

At the entrance to the park Nora slows down to go over the speed bumps and then makes her way through the lot past the neat rows of parked cars. She keeps driving then, past the asphalt and slowly onto the Green itself, her wheels sinking the slightest bit into the grass so that she has to push harder on the gas pedal to move forward. She picks up speed, heading towards the biggest garden bed she can find. A long stretch of snapdragons and freesia sits central in the green and behind it, more flowers and the fish pond. Nora notes the colours, how the sky is starting to dusk. Only dimly aware of a groundskeeper running behind the car, she heads straight into the flower bed, coming to an abrupt stop over the tulips. Nora is thrust forward in the driver's seat, the nose of the Vauxhall inclined to the water. By the time the red-faced groundskeeper has caught up, onlookers are assembled and Nora is wading into the pond with blood from a gash on her forehead matting her hair.

"Come up here, Ms.," the groundskeeper calls tentatively, stepping onto the pond bank and extending his hand. Nora stays put, waist-deep in the pond, with no intention of going any farther, no intention of drowning or of saving herself. She watches the crowd watching her, people on their after-dinner walks, mostly women with children whom they have half hidden behind their skirts, a few officials running out from the President's House. Nora notices one wee girl in particular, about two years old, her hair reddish like Nora's own and blowing about in the wind. "It's picking up," Nora says to the groundskeeper, who is wading in water up to his knees, his hand reaching out to take her arm. He seems to her somewhat earnest, the type of man who might be an entry hallway, a cozy space destined to take you into the heart of a lovely suburban family home. And Nora considers his hand, tries to take a step forward, her shoes sticking in the mud.

Giving in to its angle, the Vauxhall starts to roll forward, coming down the dirt bank. With a splash it settles into the water, knocking Nora and the groundskeeper backwards. "Christ," he says, standing up, the grill of the car directly in front of him. Then, "Ms.," and again, "Ms.," his arms reaching frantically into the muddy silt. Nora, just slightly behind him up to her neck in water, treading ever so slowly, says, "Over here, I'm over here."

"Come on," he pleads, but she shakes her head and continues to tread water, moving her arms in wide open circles. "You've gotta come out," he says, "please Ms." But she stays just out of reach, the Vauxhall barely visible now, only the crib above water, as if floating there, a slant of sunlight cutting through the trees, laid out on the broken headboard. The water is warm because of the time of year. So even as the sirens start getting closer, followed by the lights, Nora stays out in the fish pond. Wading, her arms swinging out around her. The crib, its spiralled handrails, a sort of ladder, if she should choose to get out.

The Last of It

List of things to do, rolled up in trouser pocket (yours):

Take letters, parcel to post
George Street Café 12:30
p./u thank-you card fer Moira
groceries, wine
throw self in Liffey/check flight schedule
(dinner at flat 8 P.M.?)

Note on table, tight, angular handwriting (his):

Sarah —
Gone to Guinness Brewery for tour and free stout. Sleep well? Please make bed (Moira coming home for lunch, she thot not to wake us, left £10 on counter for wine)—could you? Red wine, French bread and capers, also Parmesan, if none in fridge. Also, call Brendan to confirm dinner. Thanx, Richard.
P.S. fucking rain.

Fucking rain.
Drizzle at this point, which is noon at the earliest. Grey, another shit Dublin day. It's been like this since you arrived two weeks ago. Still, the chill in this flat, the absolute lack of any kind of

mod cons, is enough to force you out into the streets regardless of the weather. And even if that isn't enough, there's the idea of Moira, who'll be back for lunch any minute, tired from the gallery, wanting her flat to herself. Best just to open the window and wash your hair by hanging your head out into the weather and under the gutter. Easier, at any rate, than trying to haul hot water up ten flights of stairs from the laundry. Easier and more efficient in the end. A quick survey of the dingy apartment for yesterday's blouse and trousers turns up nothing. Find list, get cracking. There are errands to be done and a plane to catch tomorrow afternoon. Or not. So many things hanging in the balance. Wash your hair? Jump out the window while you're at it, or save self for Liffey? Under a large beige towel near the window, the silk blouse and black trousers confer. Next to them, a pile of letters and parcels to post.

Letters and parcels to post.
Shouldering a blue umbrella you flip through the envelopes on the walk to South Anne Street postal station. Most of them addressed to the university, reports and research, more reports. A letter to your mother on the Prairies, the last line being "I don't want to leave Ireland this time." The thought of it pitting in your stomach all over again.

"There's nothing wrong with Canada," Moira snapped two days after you'd arrived here. And you agreed, cited the good economy, weather varied enough to inspire conversation, well-towered cities, two notable mountain ranges, and the middle of the country rolling itself out like a quilt.

"So why," Moira queried, "would you want to stay?"

"History."

"History?" she said.

"A country with this much history allows you to find your place in it. There's only so much of that at home."

You hand over to the postman a parcel filled with copied gallery documents and another with Richard's smaller souvenirs. You set a letter to your sister Hannah down on the counter—this will be the fifth letter you've sent her detailing complaints about accommodation, research hassles, your lack of interest in Richard and his tourist frenzy. At the counter in the post office you draw a smiley face on Hannah's envelope, trying to fool her as well as yourself. "Everything is smashing," you say, looking at the sloppy circle, the stupid ink-drawn grin. On the other side of the counter the postmaster raises his brows. Once everything is posted you check your watch, head out to O'Connell, late for your meeting at The George Street Café.

The George Street Café.
The café is as busy as ever, everyone huddled around coffee tables, holding white china cups while smartly dickey-bowed wait staff zoom around and between the crowd. When you lived in Ireland four years ago, doing a year of your undergraduate degree at Trinity, you'd come to The George Street after class to study. You'd come with Aileen, Daragh and Daniel, who were also taking art history. Now Aileen is working in London and once you'd started your M.A. you lost touch with the guys. It would have been great to have stayed with one of them instead of Moira. That said, it would have been better if you and Richard could have afforded a hotel, or if Richard hadn't come at all.

You sit at a table near the back wall of the café and survey the room. No sign of Brendan's friend, his name gone out of your head. You're an hour late, which serves you right for dawdling along the quays, for standing there so long you nearly became a roost for the pigeons. He would have been an important person to meet, a professor of history at Trinity, a good resource for the thesis. "The Art of Dublin City, 1890-1910," he'd repeated over the phone. "That period is interesting." Then he'd rattled off a few names of relatively obscure historians whose books might be helpful. You're sorry you missed him, suppose respected academics don't sit alone in college crowds, waiting for tardy guests.

Walking down Capel Street you swing your new oxblood handbag, a spontaneous purchase last week at a Grafton Street shop. But stepping in a puddle you stop suddenly. You're wearing the wrong shoes. It's the kind of thing that throws you these days. Not that it matters. Pick up the pace. No one to notice: Richard at Guinness, Moira at lunch, and no professor at The George Street Café to care. Oxblood and brown loafers. Brendan would notice. It's always the artists you should watch out for. Add to errands: change shoes. Then call Brendan about dinner. And remember, Richard had asked you to make the bed.

Make the bed.
Shit, make bed. Still lopsided when you left. Richard had thrown all the blankets over you until you woke, nearly suffocated, to the clang of an alarm clock with brass bells. You'd dragged yourself out from under the layers slow as a snail. But stepping out of bed, the permafrost of the floor was shock enough to make you want to crawl back in. Once back at the flat you notice Richard's side of the bed is bare, just wrinkles of white sheet, the duvets heaped over on your side where, getting out of bed, he left them. A few pale stains mark the sheets from making love the night before. "Make the bed," meaning change the bed. Last night "sshhh" meant make love quietly, close your

mouth, don't creak the boxspring. "Guests, we are guests, you don't leave come stains on your host's bedsheets."

"Even if her flat is a kip?" you asked.

"Yes," Richard replied, "we are guests. And the day after tomorrow," he'd specified, "we are leaving. Let's not ruin it now."

Ruin it? Your relationship with Moira? Your relationship? You've not spent more than an hour at a time with Moira. She and Richard were always off at some Site of Monumental Cultural Import: an Arran textile mill, a Waterford glass factory. Moira giving him the first class, first rate, climb-aboard-the-Moira-Irish-cliché-Express tour. "Just like the old days," she said, meaning when she was a student of Richard's doing her undergraduate degree in Vancouver, meaning the days he showed her around the city to be hospitable.

"Stanley Park by bicycle!" Moira had nostalgically remembered on your first night here. "Oh and the art gallery, and ooohhh," clapping her hands together, "remember those matching 'whale of a time' shirts from the aquarium!" Maybe he loves Moira, you think. Maybe it's the fact that she looks up to him, or maybe her idiocy is interesting. Maybe he still has an orca slapping its tail fins against a wave emblazoned on a shirt in his bottom drawer. He'd said they'd dated. He'd said she'd studied with him at Simon Fraser University. *With him?* you think now, *or under him?* It's probably all the same. You change and make the bed. You call Brendan.

Brendan.
"Brendan."
  "Sarah?"
  "Yep."

"Hey, you missed Professor Keane—I ran into him on George Street." Brendan is an artist from Kilronan. You met when you were both at Trinity. When he speaks he sounds like he's just stepped out of a Synge play. You have to concentrate to make out exactly what he's saying.

"Yeah, sorry about that. Errands and all, I was late. Listen, can you make it for dinner tonight? It's our last night in."

"Yeah, wouldn't miss it."

"Eightish at Moira's."

"Right then."

Brendan hates Moira, he calls her a git. And he isn't big on Richard either. But Richard is all over him. Brendan's hippy west-of-Ireland paint-me-pulling-my-curragh-up-onto-the-shore mien is something Richard was fascinated by immediately. You'd gone to dinner with Brendan on your second night in, Richard complaining that you'd gone for an Italian meal in Dublin. By the time the fettucini arrived he was begging Brendan to say things in Irish, marvelling at the language as if it were some kind of magic trick. If Richard had said one more word at that point you would have killed him. So now you've called Brendan as instructed, you've set him up so that Richard can maul him and you can sit through dinner feeling appalled. Somewhere in your pocket the list: Groceries. Wine.

Wine.

You head over to the ILAC Centre. Once there you scuttle through the aisles looking for wine. Too much to choose from, but some fifty quid later you have two French Pinot Noirs, a Chianti and a Cabernet for Moira. California wine, Richard said, was always her thing. It doesn't even irk you that he knows this. The friendly salesgirl at the checkout places every bottle into its own brown bag and then she rebags those inside another brown bag before placing them into two larger, flimsy-looking plastic bags with handles that press into your palms. You thank her and she tilts her head trying to place your accent.

The groceries are only one floor up in Dunnes. Easy in theory, if one takes an escalator, but not so grand in the end because in actuality the edge of the step catches the plastic bags you've set down beside you, tearing the bottoms of the bags when, at the top of the escalator, you bend down to pick them up. Holding the bottoms of the bags, you head into the supermarket towards the grocery carts. You pick a trolley and push it towards the aisles, irritated that Richard couldn't do all this between the Guinness Brewery and his Walking Tour of Dublin, Day 10. With your right hand you root around in your pants pocket for the list.

List.
List of things Richard isn't interested in changing. As articulated in previous diatribes (his):

> *his professorship*
> *his residence*
> *his Gap-meets-Sally Ann coordinates*
> *his wispy 1970s John Denver haircut*
> *his inability to grasp what's really happening in a relationship*
> *his desire to be told same*
> *his irritation with your predisposition to list*

List.
List of things you're interested in changing, as written out two days ago in a Hilroy notebook (yours):

your tendency to research beyond the scope of your subject
your intake of sweets
your need to map things out on paper and pin them to the wall
your predictable tan-on-brown wardrobe
your weak abs
your residence
your inability to climb out of a rut

A rut.

You root around the aisles for capers and French bread. For a laugh, you pull a few boxes of cereal from the shelf and chuck them into the cart. They're a reminder of the night you and Richard made love without saying anything but the names of cereals; not even groaning was allowed, just the enunciation of words off boxes. How funny on your last night here to give Richard ten or so boxes of cereal. An amusing farewell should you hoist yourself into the river. Briefly you imagine him standing pale and shaken at Customs, the guards there letting him declare Trix and Cheerios, the Irish version of Frosted Flakes, because he tells them about you, all of them near crying. "Applejacks," he'd sigh, thinking of the orgasm. "Applejacks," sorry he ever took you for granted, sorry he'd been such a twit.

One Vancouver morning not too long ago, Richard said that he was leaving. He even started to pack his clothes. But in the end he stayed because, as he put it, he liked your company, how you never complained about his stodgy ways, his quiet descent into middle age. You remember he unpacked his bags. He waited for you to say "stay" and when you didn't, he said it for you. Three weeks later when you told him you had to go to Dublin, when you reminded him your thesis was due in two months, he said he wanted to go too. You said, "There's no point," you said you had a mountain of work to do. But he packed his bags anyway, called Moira and announced he'd arranged for a place to stay. He said "begosh and begorra" three times on the way to the airport even though you told him to stop. He brought five rolls of film. The second day here, standing on the island in the middle of O'Connell Street with a laptop computer, he went to the *Irish Times* web page. He had you wave in the direction of the "Dublin Live" camera. Then he refreshed the web page. There you were, two touristy nerds in the middle of O'Connell Street waving at something you couldn't see. Richard e-mailed the web-photo to friends and family. He said, "Now I know why you love it here." Then he went into a chip shop and asked for two portions. You ate on the concrete in a light rain. Afterwards he walked you back to the library so he could go off on a tour of Kilmanham Gaol. He said "Bye, sweet lassie" in an obnoxious brogue when you parted. And that wasn't the last of it.

The last of it.
Now, groceries in hand, you try again to find the list of things to do from this morning. Was it a question or a definitive? Jump in Liffey? Jump in Liffey. Leave Richard and his flamboyant red-haired friend. Let them sit in her shitty flat and mull over what happened. Let them wonder long into the night what, exactly, went wrong. Was that on the list as well? You can't remember. And what to do with these groceries? You step outside the Dunnes store into the tiled hallway of the shopping centre. Overhead a large clock face looms, its huge brass hands indicating 4:20 P.M. And you with your legions of bags, the plastic handles pulling, the bottoms torn, all these cereal boxes.

Suppose you take the bags over the bridge into the river with you and the bags keep you afloat? Suppose you're slowly skirted down the Liffey, the current taking you, and you're left floating because there's more air than cereal in these boxes? Suppose you get halfway up onto the rail and leave the bags on the bridge? Maybe you'd see someone—lady, man, orphan—grab the bags, the wine. Thirty quid in good Pinot Noir gone and you're so thirsty you're drinking the Liffey. And the handbag, new but altogether wrong with most of your shoes. Accessories lost and floating through Irish canals forever. Jump in Liffey? Was it ever a question? The list—hand rummaging through bag—is apparently lost.

Lost.

Damn Capel Street. That obscure short-ended street ending arbitrarily, running in and out along the quays. Damn your short-sightedness. Should have hailed a taxi. And these bags all but severing your hands in half. "Here I am," you say out loud, as if you still can't figure out how you got back here after so many years. "Here I am," you think, in this city, having been here before, having lived here to study Irish art. Now you wonder if you ever really went home. All the years in between you studied this country through books, you tried to work out a way to get back here. But that was before Richard, before his mundane imperatives and your acquiescence.

You can never go home again. That's what you thought when you left Canada to study in Dublin four years ago. And when your year was up, and you went back to Vancouver, you fooled yourself into thinking that Dublin was home. But now you realize you're just another foreigner, a woman who can't even navigate the quays. But if Richard is home, if that's what you've let home become, how can you leave him? That man gone to Guinness, burying you in bedsheets and duvets. Richard, as predictable as a set itinerary in a small tourist town:

you go to the church and nod at the architecture
you have lunch at a diner/café
you visit Old City Hall to walk past the statuary
you buy a postcard
you board the bus that picks you up exactly where and when
it should.

Where and when it should.
You've been standing on an unfamiliar street for over an hour. Once again it starts to rain. You want to take a taxi but can't afford it. The cost of living here again is apparent. Simply seen, it is the cost of wine and capers, overseas tuition. It is the ability to be alone. You're never quite a citizen with your flat-as-the-prairies accent. Always landed, migratory, unsettled.

You walk a few more blocks, trying to get reoriented. You find yourself under the arch of Christchurch Cathedral, which means you've walked too far, have skirted the south bank of the Liffey. Above the cathedral, its solid mass structure, the sky arcs like an umbrella, the church spires like spokes needling into the grey. This fucking rain, drizzle, godforsaken country. Expelling you from its rivers before you have a chance to get there. Without a map you can't even find the quays. This city bringing you here, halfway across town, to the smallness of self against sky, bricks, history. You with wine, capers, cereal and wet, stringy hair. Shortsighted and apathetic even about this. Note in hand the whole time. *Throw self in Liffey.* Definitive. Followed by a question: *dinner at flat 8 P.M.?*

Dinner at flat 8 P.M.?
You put your hands under what can be mustered of hot water. Namely, a kettle of boiled water plus cold Ballygowan from the

The Last of It

bottle on the counter. DeDannan is still playing in the tape player; everyone must have just left. Note on the kitchen table, thin scrawls in blue ink. Contents (his):

> S.
> *Gone to Brendan's—he has heat. Bring wine, capers, etc.*
> *Also, could you call airlines to confirm departure????*
> *Brendan's: #5 Rathgar Road, near Harold's Cross*
> *he says you've been there (taxi? Moira says £5.)*
> *See ya soon.*
> > *Richard*
> *P.S. Guinness good.*
> > *R.*

R.

Note on kitchen table, scrawled on back of crumpled wet list (yours):

> *Richard: Bread, wine on counter,*
> *cut my hands to shreds (bags—).*
> *Went for walk.*
> *Liffey.*

Liffey.

Still cold, still raining, and now it's evening and you're standing near Tara Street Station. Here, quick ripples move across the river that divides North and South Dublin. You look down the quays at the series of bridges and roads that cross over the waterway: O'Connell Street Bridge, Ha'penny Bridge and so forth. People cross over the bridges in the distance and for a while you watch them, wonder at them, wonder if they feel as marked as you do by the difference between the life they'd hoped for and what life has turned out to be.

There are no guardrails here, only chest-high stone walls to deter the passerby. Easy enough to climb over if one chose not to jump off a bridge. That is, if slipping over the side wall is more appealing. All the options, really: jump in Liffey, find a way to stay in Dublin, fly home tomorrow. Learn to love Richard again or leave him. And no guardrails, just years of manoeuvring around rivers to teach you how not to fall in. Call airlines, go to Brendan's, drink wine and laugh or cry. Fly back to Vancouver. Finish the thesis, decide to call somewhere home. Or throw the right leg up and over the edge, follow through full-bodied. In this handbag, a ticket without question marks. Applejacks and milk at the flat. Half a million people passing by the Liffey every day, and you only one of them. There's work to be done, you suppose. Matters to be muddled through. Best maybe to just stand here a while, watch the Liffey lapping up against the stone walls, water eddying under the bridge before finding the current and carrying on.

At the Bus Stop
in Love with the Idea

AT THE BUS STOP IN LOVE with the idea of a love you amble into like you would a bus. The kind of love that simply arrives one sunny day while you're waiting at the side of the road, its doors swinging open like arms. Carole wanted a love that would move forward under the power of a mechanism she didn't need to understand; she had a general mistrust of mechanics, the finer points. She simply liked things to work.

That morning, the 15A sloshed up to the curb and splashed everyone in sight. The man under the umbrella, holding out his arm, got it the worst. Carole spied him shaking the water off his brogues with brisk ankle kicks.

"*It takes a different sort of fellow,*" she said, surprised to have voiced her thoughts out loud.

He turned around to face her, making sure she had been addressing him.

"Sorry?"

"I said," she smiled, "*It takes a different sort of fellow.*"

He raised his eyebrows then boarded the bus. When they were settled in neighbouring seats, Carole leaned across the aisle to him and tapped him on the shoulder of his grey raincoat.

"I meant the argyle."

"Argyle?"

"Argyle," she pointed. "Your socks. Never really seen in Dublin, certainly not in July."

"Really?" He smiled politely one last time and turned towards the window.

Carole pulled a book out of her bag and set it on her lap, but instead of reading she looked around. All of the morning crowd seemed wet and grumpy. There were familiar faces, mostly eight A.M. regulars, umbrellas propped up against the backs of their seats. More and more these days, people were sporting pinned white ribbons on their lapels. Carole started to count how many people boarded the bus wearing them. Mostly it was women. The rain had yet to abate—it had been falling now for the entire month—and some people were predicting it would stay until the end of the summer. Still, at least the ceasefire in the North was holding. Ever hopeful, pedestrians and commuters made their way through Dublin, pale bows fixed firmly on their coats.

The bus jerked forward, continuing to edge its way through the traffic down Rathmines Road. Up ahead there was a stretch of roadworks to navigate through. Carole hated the wending, how the bus stopped and started, the shouts of the work crew. Across the aisle, the fellow, his hair slicked back in that "man from the ads" way, opened the *Irish Times*. TWO MEN ARRESTED WITH ARMS IN BALLYMUN was the headline of the day. These days the papers were full of the ceasefire and anything that might jeopardize it. Carole reread the headline and then, thinking about it, laughed.

"What's the harm in that?" Carole asked out loud. The woman in the red raincoat seated beside her looked around to see who was being addressed. Carole repeated herself, her head inclined towards the fellow. "What's the harm?"

"Sorry?" he looked up.

"Having arms." She tapped the paper and he folded it back over, reread the headline, said, "I see," under his breath. She figured he didn't get it, so she turned away, went back to looking out the window, waiting for her stop.

*   *   *

In love with his argyle socks. A silly thing, but Carole dreamt of them for three nights running. It was always just the socks, though, never the fellow. Socks like arms, really, and Carole up to her elbows in them. This was a new issue to take to her analyst—that, at least, was something. She was tired of all the old drivel, the "Dr. Hogan, in case you haven't noticed, this country is falling apart and I'm going with it." Sometimes she wondered if she wasn't making stuff up because it was expected. Still, she had proof enough: roadworks all along Harcourt Street, news stories depicting the Belfast riots as marching season commenced and the endless trough of rain that sent all the litter in the city sailing down the streets alongside the clogged gutters. "Anything else?" Dr. Hogan always asked at the end of a session, as if those things weren't enough. "Anything at all?" and God help her, but Carole couldn't bear to let him down.

Carole kept her eye out the next few days, watching for the fellow in the grey raincoat. She hoped he'd be at the bus stop but after a few days without seeing him she figured he was probably riding the 8:00 A.M. bus she usually managed to catch. She'd been running behind the past few mornings, barely making the 8:15. On the fourth day, she made the 8:00 and he was there, wearing a white shirt and navy suit.

"I've dreamt of your socks for three nights," she said, putting her 85p down on the driver's tray, following right behind the fellow and then into the seat beside him. As she sat down the skirt she was wearing fanned out over his leg. He eyed it self-consciously and then looked up at her.

"Really?"

"Yep. What do you think it means?"

"I haven't the slightest."

He lifted her skirt off his trousers and then looked her in the eye for the first time.

"Maybe you should buy a book? Jung or *10,000 Dream Interpretations*, something along those lines," he suggested.

Carole's fingers played with the cuffs of her cardigan. She hadn't much to say in response to that.

The fellow smiled briefly, recognizing the conversation had run its course. Turning to look up the aisle, he watched people passing through on their way to the upper level. An attractive woman started up the stairs and Carole noticed her companion was watching the blonde woman's ascent, her hip bumping up against the stairwell wall as the bus set off.

"I might ask my therapist," Carole continued, as if still in the midst of discussion, "about the dreams, but it's not really his area."

The fellow raised an eyebrow, interested. "His specialty is?"

"Analysis. I'm quite unbalanced." She said it matter-of-factly. "I go once a week and he does this sort of hypnotherapy trip."

A horn blared from somewhere in traffic, the bus swerved a bit, then the driver hit the brakes. Carole grabbed the top of the bus seat in front of her with both hands. The fellow also reached out to steady himself on the back of the seat in front of him and his hand landed squarely on Carole's. The bus driver then laid on the horn and a few seconds later, with a surge, they moved ahead in traffic and carried on. The fellow straightened his tie in spite of it being straight to begin with.

"You were saying?"

"Well," Carole hesitated, looking out the window to see what had happened, "that I'm mad." She looked back over at him, continued: "Insane actually, and that I go to hypnotherapy where I'm often transported back to the Bronte novels of my youth, excepting that my doctor, Dr. Hogan, isn't very well read and he thinks that a Mr. Heathcliff has in fact done me quite wrong." Carole turned back towards the window trying to figure out what had caused the bus to swerve.

"Hypnotherapy?" the fellow clarified.

"Exactly."

"Using a gold watch?" he volunteered.

"Pen, actually." She smiled over at him. "Back and forth like this." She moved her finger from side to side in front of his eyes. Carole could tell he was amused.

The fellow nodded his head up and down slowly, pretending his eyelids were getting heavy, then broke into an easy smile when she wiggled her finger. They sat in silence for a few stops before he turned to face her again.

"Basic black, I'm afraid." He pulled his trouser leg up and nodded towards the exposed ankle.

"A safe bet," she replied, pulling on the Next Stop cord and making her way carefully to the side doors.

*　*　*

In love with the idea of a woman who dreams about his socks. Sean watched for the argyle-sock woman at the bus stop the next morning. He'd thought about her all the previous day at the office. Thought about her while shuffling papers around, adding up figures, even while flirting with Maureen, the frumpy, middle-aged secretary who he knew wanted to ask him out.

It takes a different sort of fellow, the woman had said. Sean had always felt rather regular, a white-bread, beans-on-toast sort of man. It was a psychological complex that had arrived smack dab with his certificate in accounting and his brother's emigration to America. This woman was quirky and direct, not your typical Irish girl. He found her quite intriguing.

The next morning Sean spied her coming out of the snack shop across the street from the bus stop. She had on the same yellow skirt and black cardigan as yesterday. Her short brown hair was held back by silver clips above her temples. She smiled when she saw him and came across the street, said "Hi."

"Sean," he said, thrusting out his hand. "Hi," she said again, and in a quiet voice, "I'm Carole." She shook his hand and then turned, checking to see if the bus was coming down the road.

They waited side by side for a few minutes until a bus pulled out of a stop down the way and Carole stepped out to check the number. A few people held out their arms and what turned out to be the 14 pulled up to the curb. Carole and Sean moved back towards the shelter to wait for the 15A.

"The socks?" he asked, wanting to start the conversation on a personal level. "Any more dreams?"

Carole laughed and, in spite of wanting to pursue the conversation, turned her attention to the clogged gutters. She was off work at the shop today for another session with Dr. Hogan. As with confession, she was already preparing a mental list of what to say. Thought she'd start with how she was fixated with a stranger from the Rathmines bus stop. How everything about him seemed exact and perfect and in place. Carole imagined how she would start the session. "Forgive me Good Shrink for I have sinned, I'm mad for argyle." Chances were, though, that Dr. Hogan would craftily bring it all back round to *that*. "Good enough with Argyle Man," he'd say, tapping his pen on the metal clipboard, "but back to business shall we, what about *you*?"

The 15A was a block up the street and as it came closer Carole felt that same old apprehension, a tightening in her chest. What were the mechanics of carrying on? How to do it? She went over it in her head. The bus will stop, you'll get on, pay the fare. It will not pull away without you. You will have enough change, and the lot of you will go forward. The streets are not littered with paper bags concealing bombs, and you will not get off the bus, turn the corner towards Wicklow Street and fall off the face of the earth. At worst there will be more rain and clogged gutters. At the end of your day you will unlock your door and go quietly inside.

Sean watched Carole examining the gutters. He was trying to think of something else to say. He felt like an eejit for trying to start a conversation with socks as the central topic. When she moved to the curb he followed her. After a minute the bus pulled up and together they queued up for it, but at the last second, Sean moved back so that a woman and her baby could get on ahead of him. Once out of the queue, he ended up waiting beside the door until most of the other people had boarded. The bus was so overcrowded that he had to stand in the aisle. At the top of Grafton he turned to wave at Carole before he got off but he couldn't make her out in the crowd.

The radio was always on in Dr. Hogan's office. Carole sat in the waiting room and tried to tune out RTE. A warm front was making its way up from the south, they said, rain for the next few days, maybe clearing up after the weekend. "And in headline news: the rate of heart disease in Ireland is increasing. A girl in

Liscarroll has gone missing. And today the European Union promises development money to the North." The newscaster's voice was low and comforting, "First, in the headlines: a UVF faction group has claimed responsibility for two recent bomb threats to the Stormont government. Mo Mowlam fears there is little hope now for decommissioning."

Carole looked over to Moira, Dr. Hogan's secretary, but Moira, oblivious, was flipping through some files. Carole wanted to ask her to turn the radio off but she didn't. Instead she concentrated on the weather. A warm front. On its way up from the south.

*   *   *

At the office window in love with the idea of instability, the kind of instability that comes from not knowing what's going to happen next. Sean had always relied on routines, a careful accounting with narrow margins. He'd thought he wanted a relationship where everything added up, a system of whole numbers, no decimals, no fractions. But he had to admit that Carole had thrown him off guard. He wanted to ask her out but he didn't know where to begin.

Looking out the window onto Grafton Street, Sean watched a glut of summer tourists crowding around two young boys who were singing "Danny Boy" off key. Stepping back he checked his reflection, noticed there were muffin crumbs on his lapel. He stood over the waste bin and brushed them off. Maureen, on the phone at the desk beside him, was giving figures to Rob, the Head Accounts Manager at the record store's main office in London. HMV Dublin's sales were beyond expectation. Things were looking good. If only he could find a way to get off on the right foot with that woman from the bus, then, at least, there'd be more to his life than sales projections, promotional freebies and an office with a decent view.

On the bus home that day Sean realized he was looking around for Carole and then thought he'd better reign himself in. After all, he didn't really know anything about her. And therapy was a sure sign of someone to stay away from unless you fancied a bit of volunteer work on your off hours. But coming up towards Leinster, a bus shelter advert caught his eye. It featured a sharp-looking guy with pearly teeth and a cellular phone. BE DIRECT it said in bold letters, then in smaller letters, Direct Cellular. Sean's was the next stop.

The next morning there was a fairly large crowd at the bus stop. Most of the commuters, including Carole, huddled under the shop's awnings to avoid the rain. When Carole saw Sean standing by the road under his umbrella, she walked over to him. He was looking down the street.

"Socks again," she said, getting drenched in the rain.

"Really?" He was relieved, glad she'd initiated conversation. He held the umbrella up over both their heads and the rain poured down the slope of it, funneling right onto his back.

"On my arms, up to here," she gestured.

Sean moved sideways to face her, adjusting the umbrella so that Carole had better cover from the rain, exposing his back altogether. He noticed a light flowery smell about her, like roses. Unconsciously he moved his face closer to hers.

"Do you think it means anything?" she asked, furrowing her brow and looking up at the mess of the umbrella's spokes. "About us, I mean? You know, considering the volume of argyle dreams and all that, not to mention the shared bus route." Angling her head sideways, she gave him a quizzical look.

At the Bus Stop in Love with the Idea

Clearing his throat, he felt colour rising to his cheeks. "It's certainly possible," he said.

Carole ducked out from under the umbrella and made her way to the bus. Sean hadn't even seen it arrive. He followed her on board and when he realized there was nowhere they could sit together, he stood in the aisle beside her seat. The bus pulled into traffic, surging ahead every now and again and then abruptly stopping. Sean was rocking back and forth in the aisle. Carole looked at him swaying back and forth and without meaning to, she laughed. He reminded her of the old clock in the hall outside her flat, its big brass pendulum swinging the minute hand around in perfect time, day after day. The wholly dependable gong on the hour. Sean was just like that, she thought, even his swaying as the bus manoeuvred through the roadworks was evenly paced.

Just before they got to Carole's stop, Sean started in, saying more to his shoe than to her, "Is it possible you might have time for lunch today, or maybe tomorrow?"

"I'd like that," Carole said, and then added, "today's good."

"Shall we meet?" He was starting to feel a bit formal, tried to relax his grip on the overhead bar.

"Okay," Carole smiled up at him. "There's a café next to work, I'm at the Sweater Shop on Wicklow?"

He nodded, could sort of picture a window display full of Arran knits.

"Well, Cornucopia, the restaurant's called, it's just past my shop."

"Right," he smiled, feeling like the whole of the bus was watching them. "One okay, or half-one?"

"One," she said, and then, to his relief, she slipped out under his arm and shouldered her way to the door.

The restaurant was fairly packed with only a few free stools along the far wall. It was buffet style and people were queued up with trays; hot dishes were being handed over the counter to waiting customers by a few serving staff. Sean opted for the lentil loaf and Caesar salad. Carole had spinach pie and potatoes. Once served they squeezed, trays overhead, between a row of seated customers, and set themselves up under a bulletin board plastered with colourful posters. Sean watched Carole as she lifted their plates, pulled out the trays, and walked them across the room, setting them on the pile of trays that were stacked under a wide counter. He thought, looking at her, that she was really quite beautiful, he even allowed himself to imagine that there might be a future for them. Years from now they might be walking out along the strand and maybe the look of her then, or a gesture she might make as she turned around to face him, would bring him back to this moment. *It takes a different sort of fellow.* Which is exactly what he wanted to be.

"You live in Rathmines?" he began once they were settled.

"Yep. Grosvenor Square."

"Nice."

"Bit expensive. You?" She picked up one of her small boiled potatoes and popped it into her mouth.

"Leinster."

"Um."

"So," Sean surveyed the bulletin board on the wall above them, "how's sock therapy going?"

"All's well with the socks," she said, smiling.

"Good." He looked her right in the eye and said it again. "Good." He really meant it, was building up to asking her what exactly was wrong.

After they finished their meals he felt courageous enough to ask. In answer to his nervous question Carole said, "Anything can happen. You can wake up one morning alone. People die or they leave you. Just walk out one day without so much as a note, burnt toast left on a plate next to the jam and butter. Bombs go off. Or you yourself can come down with something incurable. And there's fires, theft, getting shot. And even without that, just the idea of it and you start to fail at things, question everything like you've just misplaced something, keys for example, objects needed for the everyday."

Sean wiped his mouth. He was feeling a bit red in the face again and he wondered if anyone was listening. Carole was still caught up in her thoughts. Sean turned away, looked around the restaurant as if looking for a cue. He didn't get what she was saying; he'd expected that maybe she'd have said a parent had died, something unfortunate that would be easy to understand.

"It's like," Carole concluded, "like being given something and you don't know what it is, how to use it." She managed to look Sean right in the eye. "Days when I can't even leave the house."

* * *

At the sweater shop in love with the idea of a routine. The kind of routine that's automatic, no thinking required, no lump in your throat, just the progression of a day in expected increments, a day that unfurls itself without any bumps in the road. Carole imagined that having a routine would be like knitting, the work so familiar that you're barely aware of the fact that you're doing it. Knit two, purl two and again and again. One's progress, the real shape of things, only evident when you find yourself near the end.

All afternoon, Carole thought about Sean. She pulled a crew-neck sweater out of a new shipment of sweaters and laid it out, front down, on the counter. She crossed one arm of the sweater over the other, then pulled the top half back to make a perfect rectangle. Then she set it aside and pulled another out of the box. Sean had said she should come by the office sometime, that if she asked downstairs at the cash registers, they'd call him down to meet her.

Back at work, Sean stared out the window. He couldn't shake the idea that something about Carole was just too odd. But what, he wondered, was the danger in that? She was funny and outgoing, and she really was quite beautiful. He looked over at Maureen who was on the phone with head office. She winked at him and waved the pen in her hand, then went on relaying sales figures to London. Maybe, Sean thought, this wasn't the time to start in with someone who might be a bit unbalanced: the country was doing well, the GDP in Ireland just exceeded that of Britain, and HMV was opening shops everywhere from Monaghan to Clare. Sean was going to be busy. Why chance it with Carole when things were at an even keel?

*　　*　　*

Carole hadn't seen Sean in over a week. She'd even stopped by HMV. The salesgirl phoned upstairs but after hanging up she told Carole that Sean was out. Carole figured Sean had started catching the 7:45 or 8:15. Up early for a change, she pulled on her slicker and made the bus stop at 7:40. Sean was there, huddled safely under his large black umbrella, squinting at the onslaught of traffic coming down Rathmines Road. Carole noticed a few of his umbrella spokes had popped out from under the fabric, giving the thing a caved-in appearance on one side. She thought about the mechanics of an umbrella: simple support frame, axis, open, close, open, close. But there must be something else.

A latch or something to hold it in place or lock it in, she wasn't sure. The 7:45 15A trundled down Rathmines Road. Sean stuck out his arm. Carole moved up behind him, was about to tap his shoulder.

"*It takes a different sort of fellow.*"

He turned around, feeling caught. "Sorry?"

Carole was standing in the rain, her hair was stuck to her head and rain drops were beading on the end of her nose.

"I said," she was louder this time, "*It takes a different sort of fellow.*"

Sean smiled unconvincingly, thinking of the last time he'd seen her at Cornucopia. He felt bad for avoiding her. He'd taken her number at the restaurant and said he'd call, and he knew she'd come by HMV but every time he went to ring her, he changed his mind.

"Different sort," he smiled, shifting his umbrella to his left hand and with his right, pulling up his pant leg to reveal thin navy socks. "Laundry," he smiled again, feeling anxious. "Er, sorry, Carole, I didn't uh, I—feel a bit like a—a sod, really." He was biding time and she knew it. She'd suspected right there and then at Cornucopia that he'd been overwhelmed. This is how it went with people, how it went with Dr. Hogan—they wanted straight answers for difficult questions, they wanted mapped-out scenarios. "Sometimes just the idea of something is enough to scare you." That's what Carole, in a moment of clarity, had said to Dr. Hogan. Still, after lunch, Sean had taken her number, he'd said he'd call. And after walking her back to the shop, he'd told her he thought she was amazing.

So, standing at the bus stop, Carole considered what had passed. She considered her options, and then, once decided, brought her knee up, smiled sweetly, and kicked Sean firmly in the shin. It takes a different sort, she thought, moving back from the curb, and around the sidewalk puddles. Under the shop awning she folded her arms, waited for the next bus.

Sean boarded the 15A and once seated, he tried to wipe the muddy bits off his pant leg. There would definitely be a bruise, that much was certain. The bus pulled away from the curb and through his window Sean saw that Carole was still under the awning, probably waiting 15 minutes to avoid having to travel into town with him. As the bus pulled out, the rain started coming in heavy waves, Sean couldn't see past the grey sheets of run-off streaming down the window, would have to guess at where his stop was. Up front the bus driver's windshield wipers were slapping away at full speed. At best, Sean could glimpse the bright red or yellow of a shop's awning, and that only in the clear moments.

Halfway to town the guy seated beside Sean started to cough, he went into a sort of a fit, his hands hardly covering his mouth. Sean wanted to say "All right?" and he thought maybe he should pat him hard on the back or something, but he couldn't bring himself to do it. The bloke got quite red in the face. His scuffed hard hat fell off his lap onto the floor, went rolling under the bus seat towards the front.

The impact came without warning, threw some people out of their seats and into the aisle. Sean knocked his chin on the railing in front of him and drove his shin into the bottom bracket of the seat. The guy next to him dropped his hard hat again. "Everybody all right? All right now?" the driver shouted, undoing his seat belt and looking back at the passengers. A few people came down the stairs from the upper level. Outside, the sound of the rain pounded on the roof of the bus. People were standing up, seemingly unhurt, everyone sort of milling about.

"I need your names," the driver shouted, "and phone numbers on this clipboard." He held it over his head. "If you feel okay, and want to get off, sign this first!"

"There's an old man up here needs help," a voice yelled from the stairwell, and the bus driver and a young female passenger both made their way up the stairs. A few people headed for the door and Sean followed, signing the clipboard left on the fare tray. The bus had gone up a curb and hit a fire hydrant, and the bottom step of the bus was flooded. Water was streaming out from the hydrant on all sides. The rain itself had somewhat abated but the streams of water from the hydrant were gushing full tilt. Sean got drenched as he jumped sideways, trying to avoid the bottom step. He held onto the door flap until the last second.

Carole's bus stopped and the driver hung up his radio, turned towards the passengers and announced a road closure due to accident. "Anyone going to the Green, Grafton et cetera should get off here and walk, I'm to go left onto George." Carole got up and made her way to the door, stepping out onto the curb and getting her bearings. About a half-block up, the 15A sat angled on the road, the front end tilted up on the sidewalk, water blasting in all directions from the fire hydrant. People were milling around the bus driver, who was shaking his head. When Carole was almost alongside the bus she saw Sean, limping a bit, his umbrella still wonkier than she remembered and his suit sopping wet. He had a grin from ear to ear, was twenty feet down the street, looking right at her.

Turning to look back at the bus, Sean had spotted Carole coming towards him. It occurred to him that maybe he could detail the accident, give her a full account, he was hoping they could laugh about the shin. Sean waved her way once, then leaned forward, still waving. Maybe this, he thought, was the moment he would return to. Carole coming toward him from the crowded road side, turning to him and heading his way.

After weeks of cloud and rain the sun hit the roadway. Looking up, Carole saw an ochre light spread out across the park. It went up the glassy side of the shopping centre, it fanned out towards the Liffey. The rain stopped. It was simultaneous. The sun and Carole's decision to keep walking. As she passed Sean she threw one look over her shoulder and then kept going, across the street and straight ahead towards the sweater shop. There'd been an accident and she'd missed it; some of her faith was restored. The rain had finally abated, and even though there were orange-jacketed men up on Harcourt doing street repairs, even though there were holes in the road, Carole had passed them without incident. Progress was at hand.

Across the street, Sean, standing in a puddle, was still watching Carole, thought about picking up and going after her. He didn't. Instead he headed up to work annoyed at the squelching sounds his soaked loafers made with every step. Then, looking down Grafton, he saw Carole turn the corner at Wicklow—only a glimpse of her, but it was Carole to be sure. I should call out her name, he thought, she'd come back if I did. Sean broke into a run, half flailing, his briefcase banging up against his leg. But once he turned the corner, he stopped. Carole carried on in the distance, coming in and out of view between the crowds. Sean just stood there, watched her go. Wondered about that for years, went back to it again and again.

At the Bus Stop in Love with the Idea

The Caoin Funeral

IF GRIEF COULD BE HELD, cupped even, in the well of the hands, that would be something, would approach enough. Become, at least, a quantity of loss. Better that than the sound of it—the dull blades of ice skates that cut across the pond as they come towards you. First one foot then the other, a seesaw in your sleep. Outside the snow is piled in mountains, drifts three feet high on the roof. Everything waiting.

When you'd opened your eyes the morning of the drowning the Banshee was there, in your apartment, her arm wrapped around the bedpost. There was a moment of panic. You'd reached your hand out frantically, knocking over the alarm clock, a glass, sending the book you were reading to the floor. You blinked once, then again, and she wavered, leaned in a bit, cleared her throat. She said nothing. Neither of you moved. The phone rang. On the carpet, the water from your glass was soaking in.

It started the morning of the drowning.

No, it started when the water froze over.

Black's Pond was a place you'd always gone. Growing up, you and your brother and sister went through ice skates every year. Whenever you outgrew yours another pair was bought, your mother placing an ad on the bulletin board of the IGA, sometimes getting lucky the same day. She'd paid five dollars once for a polished cream-coloured pair, even the laces clean and new-looking. Rachel by then would have grown into your old skates, or for a winter she'd wear two thick wool socks and ankle guards to keep her feet from wobbling. Lee had his black hockey skates, wore a Maple Leafs jersey, played in the Timmins Junior League. Out on the pond you'd practice your eights. Evergreen trees all around.

At the wake you looked out the window, the branch of a tree scraping against the glass, wanting in. There was a gust of wind and the snow came free of the bough. Trapped in that space between branch and window, it piled up along the pane, looking like the fake snow kids spray on glass in wave patterns; small pulses, powdered bits escaping outside the lines. You thought: symmetry. Triangle. On your mother's sideboard, the three of you in an old Christmas photo from Sears. Your hands, one on each of their shoulders. Rachel's lips tight to hide her braces.

Everyone was milling about. Your mother was making busy with the food trays: crackers, cheese, rolls and spinach dip. Someone arranged fruit pieces and a slice of cake on a plate; they must have handed the plate to you. When you finally noticed it, it was sitting precariously on your lap, ready to slide down the slope of your skirt, spill all over the carpet. You could see it, as if it had already happened.

Remember.

Tobogganing down the hill from Shub Street to Reaume. You'd been told to watch for cars. One March when you were eight and Rachel was six you forgot and, whipping down the snow-bank, you careened alongside a black Chrysler. Even with the driver's foot full on the brake, the car skidded on the ice and hit you, everyone coming to a stop in the middle of the road. Blue plastic toboggan sliding out from beneath you. Cold snow up your pant leg. You cried through ten stitches, each one looped through the skin behind your ear where your head had hit the chrome bumper. Rachel without even so much as a bruise. "She's an angel," your mother had teased, "a lucky little angel with wings."

They'd found Rachel just like that. Her wool coat open under the ice, the ivory lining fanning out around her. A satiny sheen to it. Glints of sunlight on the pond surface, blue water bobbing up out of the hole, softening the ice around it. A wound. A widening halo over her head.

At the wake you thought in names: Jim Smith, his wife Annie. And towards the fireplace, your mother Marjorie, talking to the Minics from Albert Street; and near the buffet, pointing at the Royal Dalton, beside the framed family photo, Constable Benny and Sergeant Hebb. And there was Rachel's boyfriend from twelfth grade, Fitz, she'd called him, standing awkwardly near the stack of rented fold-out chairs, a plastic cup in his hand. Marianne, Connie from the college—girls Rachel had invited over to dinner just two weeks before. Connie with mascara streaks halfway down her face. And there was Lee, coming towards you.

Names were the only sure things.

"Banshee," she'd said the second time she appeared, the night after the phone call, after the long useless hours spent in the hospital, after the doctor finally managed to send the family home. Ban-shee, drawn out for effect, making you expect a "Hello My Name Is" sticker, a spelling lesson. She'd done a few turns in the half light of the room, had come towards the bed as if she was going to take your temperature. She'd said, "I've heard you've suffered a loss." Then she was gone.

At the wake your mother's eyes had flickered, opened in recognition. Looked right over to where the Banshee was sitting, her pale hand toying with the wreath, one bent finger running over the ribbon's "We'll Miss You Rachel" lettering. The Banshee had stayed until the close of the wake. You were sure of it. No one else noticed how she walked around the room, crouched over and half lame, a scraggy-faced visage pinching the mini-quiche hors d'oeuvres. Everyone began to leave when the clock clanged away at eleven, and they processed past the three of you, Lee oblivious to everything but the handshakes, claps on the shoulder. Your mother kissed everyone on the cheek, ignoring the Banshee, going into the kitchen, noisily stacking the plates.

* * *

You have taken to your bed because it is all you can do. Grief piled up like feather-filled blankets. And now you are paralyzed, can neither pull the blankets up over your head nor slip out from under them. Your mother has come to the apartment twice this morning and you have not even gone to the door. A numbness that makes you feel brittle. At the foot of your bed the Banshee is combing snowflakes through her hair; they melt against the comb's bone teeth, wet her grey head. A curse, you think. A vision.

The Banshee has come back every night since the drowning, coming back in the flat black oil-slick of your dreams, and even when you are waking, she is there, lips curling over her teeth to greet you. This morning she unwinds herself from the footboard and sits on the edge of the bed, smoothing the quilt with one hand. Tied to this, you think, tied to this and the bed. For weeks now, without a reprieve.

"Get up and go outside," your brother said yesterday, standing in your bedroom doorway in his RCMP uniform, cap under his arm like it had been at the funeral. He gave up in the end, but raised the blinds and opened the windows a crack before going back on duty. You made a trip to the bathroom after showing him to the door, knowing it made him happy to see that you were at least walking around the apartment, to know you could heat up a can of soup if you needed to.

"How've we been?" This morning the Banshee reaches out and tweaks a toe. Tries to gather your attention. Vivid. The black on her teeth, the calcified mound of bone on the slope of her nose. A loose thread on her right sleeve.

Consider, here, the rules: Acknowledge her and you are giving in. Embracing delusions only makes them stronger. The smell of her, though. Hard to call that into creation, imagine it at all. Unearthly at the very least. Mildew twinged with rotted fruit and worse. "Fever?" she asks, her eyes trying to find yours. "Bed sores?" She moves to lift up the blankets, has her hand on the corner of the quilt. "None," you say, then clear your throat as if caught speaking aloud in an empty room.

In truth it goes back farther than you care to remember.

"Hello," you'd called out from the centre of the pond, thought maybe it was Lee coming from practice, or that a deer was mucking about in the undergrowth by the trees. You'd skated the perimeter. There it was again. A sort of cracking sound, the crisp breaking of twigs. "Hello!" You'd watched your breath funnel out in the cold. You were just past your tenth birthday and there she was. Or maybe you're making it up now. Knowing that at that moment your father was at the hardware store, going down on one knee, his hand pulling on his collar. A wild-eyed bone-thin woman in black rags walking slowly towards the pond from the treeline as he stopped breathing in the shop across town. She'd scared you so much that you'd skated to the snow bank before she was anywhere near you. You'd pulled your boots on and run home.

"The Banshee," your grandmother had told you, saying, "that's what you saw. Come to console you over the death of your father." And she talked to you about faeries as well, and the "wee green men" who used to live in the hedge near her house in county Clare. You thought there was less credibility in her Celtic stories than in the Grimm Brother tales you'd read before bedtime.

It was a short-lived joke the year after your Gran died. "Don't, Lee!" you'd tease your brother, "Or Granny will send the Banshee to get you." Making craggy claws with your hands and grabbing at him, Rachel screaming between bursts of giggles, holed up behind the big stuffed chair in the corner of the living room. Your mother had put a stop to that altogether and never said why.

And now, here she is, in your apartment, the Banshee, always popping up in an instant, hanging over you, then gone like she has come, in a blink. You could set a calendar by her. Hasn't missed a day since they found Rachel. She comes, stays for five minutes or so, moving around the room, her feet sliding across the floorboards like the skates that scissor through your sleep.

The sound of them is more than you can bear. The Banshee holding her hand out to you in that instant before she disappears. Tick, you think, and again, mentally carving thin lines into the bedpost after she goes. Tick, another day survived, the few minutes of visitation enough to keep you from napping in the afternoon, enough to keep you awake until late into the evening.

There are articles on bereavement on the bedside table, most of them from the police officers' wives. A book called *After the Burial*, an Ann Landers column clipped from the *Daily Express* sitting on top of the pile. "Dear Ann: Recently my sister died from complications related to ..." But there are no real-life dramas from *Reader's Digest* describing how under water in winter a person's mouth freezes open, lips turning a luminescent blue, how the last bubbles of breath, pearl-like, attach themselves to the underside of the ice. Break open with a sigh when they hit the warmer air, like a flower opening up to the sun. Uncomplicated. The traffic of veins. Everything neatly arranged and made apparent under the transparency of skin. Blood on its way from the heart, circling back again but coming to a stop, ice chips in the artery, small and red like rubies.

"Just checkin' up," the Banshee says. "Day twenty-two." And it makes you laugh to think she's counting. There's dry caked saliva around her lips, as if she too doesn't get out much. Her skin is a series of cracks and crevices. Her breastbone is level under the pitch of her gown. She goes out of the bedroom and into the kitchen. You wait for her to walk back in through the doorway. There's only the hum of the fridge. You push off the covers and go out, feet shocked by the cold of the linoleum. You look around. She's baiting you out of bed. Once back under the covers you realize you were hoping to find her.

The Caoin Funeral

You still can't talk about it. Lee works around it, discusses death and accidents in a clinical way. He processes it like he processed last week's robbery at the liquor store. "The assailant shot at the victim twice. The first shot hit the back wall, the second shot impacted the victim's arm, here. The assailant made away with $462 and a case of Labatt's Blue. We are in the process ..." Fixed details, all it is.

Cause of death: hypothermia. A melted spot in the ice. She slipped through on her walk to college. Was found by a group of school children in the early afternoon. Floating. Eyes open to the silvery slip of sky, her face bobbing up towards the sun, hands still in mittens, pressed up into that thin seam of air that exists between water and ice. A hallelujah gesture is what you imagine, her arms stretched out around her head, reaching into infinite space. The possibility of her somersaulting down through the silted darkness to the hard black pond bottom, unfathomable, even now.

Your mother gives in, confesses. Tells you everything from her standpoint, which is also at the foot of your bed. "I saw her at the wake," she says, telling you how she even went so far as to follow the Banshee into the kitchen, confront her once and for all. "Stay away from my children. From my house." Even picked up the Best O' the Emerald Isle tea towel off the counter, swished it in front of her as if she was trying to scatter crows from atop the fence. Had the apparition backed into the corner, was about to reach for the broom. "Put it down," the Banshee had croaked, sounding tired. "Not if my life depended—" and your mother tells you how she stopped mid-sentence, thought about it, walked out of the kitchen. "Ignore her and she'll go away," is the only advice she offers. Your mother checking every room in your apartment, even inside the closets, in cupboards, the pantry, before going home.

"Or Grandma will send the Banshee," you'd threatened when you were fourteen, making claws with your hands and holding them over your head. You'd wailed like you thought the Banshee might wail and Rachel had crawled under your parents' bed, set herself perfectly in the centre so that reaching under from either side you missed her entirely. EEEEEE you screamed, jumping up and down on the mattress until she skittered out and made for the living room where your brother was watching the Stanley Cup playoffs. EEEEEE.

*　　*　　*

Now you've spent over a month in bed, the mail spilling out of the box and even your brother, dropping off groceries, tells you this is the last time. Your mother has also given up on you. She's going to bereavement groups on Wednesday nights all the way over in Cochrane, making the drive by herself. Outside, the roads have cleared a bit and the wet brown earth is turning up in murky patches where tire tracks coalesce. The pond ice melts quickly this time of the year, breaks up into bits that disintegrate altogether in only a day or two. Think: symmetry. Instead you see all those tiny ice islands bobbing on the pond surface, moving this way and that in the wind, like sailboats blown in every direction—there too, the inevitable collision.

"Still on your laurels, I see." This morning the Banshee is busy with a tangle of hair, picking through it with her comb. When everything is in order she comes towards you like a mother would, tenderly, as if to pull the blankets up under your chin. The noise of it. First a low moan, a humming sound, then from her throat a guttural scream that fills the room, forcing you back against the headboard. She reaches her right hand out and touches your throat, ever so gently opening your mouth with her thumb, all the while keening. And out it comes from you, almost a whisper, then, as if pulled from your chest, an uneven bellowing cry. You cover your face, press your fingers hard against your eyelids, tears welling up in your hands.

Outside a patch of snow slides off the roof, thuds into what's left of a snowbank. A car drives by on the street, tires whooshing through slush. Then nothing, for the longest time. Like the pond on a spring day—the water calm, the trees still, everything coated in silence. No birds, no wind, not even a sound.

THE NOVELLA

What's Left Us

Bearing

Bearing down is the beginning of letting go. Eight months in and already there's the desire to start pushing. As if love demands a kind of suffering. As if love could make a difference at all.

On the tube approaching Paddington Station the thought first occurs to you: this is not your average fork in the road, this is the pivotal moment, the one returned to again and again. Only this time you see it coming, and this tube, troddling along, skirting subway walls, takes you closer to it. You will get off at Bayswater and within blocks that moment—concrete steps and Georgian doorway—will have arrived. There is still time to pull out pen and paper from your bag, push the black mutt's leash up past your elbow and get down to business. Pen to paper, write: organize options. Write: make list of things to do.

At Bayswater Station, Winston lopes up the two flights of steps and you trundle along behind him. It is the first bright day London has seen since winter. In the window of an Italian eatery you check your reflection, stomach protruding from beneath the blue cotton dress, unruly hair starting to escape its bun. There is no going back and even if you had thought otherwise, it is the baby that propels you forward now. How many times this past month have you found yourself standing here? How many times have you turned back? Simply and blindly we embrace our undoing. This, too, is one of life's miracles.

You might sit on his doorstep for half the day waiting. If he is out of town you might sit there through spring. He will return home from Shangri-La in early summer with his wife and two children to find you suntanned on his step nursing his baby. Again he will seduce you with talk of architecture and art, with his love of old London buildings. Only this time the baby will be colicky and you'll be cranky from having waited up for three months to see him. His wife will irritate you by her very presence and her smug look of satisfaction, her eyes bearing down on you, the gauche and flagrant proof of his infidelity. But you will be seduced nonetheless, take what he has to offer and go back to your flat in Camden Town, picking up a box of diapers and some dog food at the Corner Value Shoppe on the way. It has always been like this and why, for you, should it be any different?

Round the corner and walk the half block up to his doorstep. Steel yourself; it's time things changed.

"There'll be a baby," you say, although it's obvious.

"Is it mine?"

"Of course, Adam."

"Listen, I'm sorry, Victoria's home, shall we step outside?"

In Hyde Park he kisses you, your back against a tree. His hand on your breast, he mumbles into your neck how he's missed you, thought of you. Already he's glossed over the all-too-apparent fact of the baby. You move his hand down towards your belly and check his eyes for a reaction. He stares back at you. It's getting chilly outside and the dog has started to whine.

To get in from the wind he takes you to a small falafel bar where you drink tea and stab at the tabouli with a plastic fork. You talk formalities: when it might have happened, when the baby is due. You skirt the unskirtable issue. After a while he puts his head in his hands and tells the arborite counter, "There's no way I can leave her." You shrug, say, "I didn't expect you would," although you surprise yourself because under all the bravado you'd hoped he'd pack up and come home with you; you'd hoped he'd say it would only take him a week, that he'd at least be a convincing liar.

Sitting together at the counter along the side wall, dog tied to the newspaper stand out front, it has come to this:

"You look beautiful, pregnant like that."

"The baby is due in a month."

"How much do you need?"

He could fill ten pillow cases with twenty-pound notes and it would not undo the damage he has done today. The cook in the paper cap wipes down his pop dispenser, listens to your conversation, wipes the same nozzle again and again. By the time he has moved on to the next nozzle you've agreed on a bank account, moderate amounts of money put into it for the first five years. You stab at the last cherry tomato, decide on the Lloyds branch at Camden and head out the door amazed that you might once have loved him.

Descending the steps into Bayswater Station you shout "Heel" louder than you should and yank too hard on Winston's leash. This is not what you had wanted. But wait, there is a small jab under your right rib. Hold the handrail, stop walking; this is a reminder. Before the turnstile take out your pen and paper again. Cross out "Options," write "What is important." That is enough.

The Facts

What is important are the facts. Babies are made and born. Children are brought up in the world. It goes well or it doesn't. There was your own birth. Tugged out backwards under the bright fluorescent light of the delivery room. "There there now," all your mother could say, "there there now," because of the pain she herself was feeling, her pelvis pushed open so wide that it would be a week of sleeping with an old leather belt cinched around her hips before she could get out of the hospital bed. "There there now," and those first days in Mercy General where they passed you from nurse to mother to Aunt Clara and on to your grandmother.

Your father dropped by on the third day, tapped his hand against the glass to the nursery, probably winked or cuckooed as the nurse held you up for him to see. He was not one easily won over, your mum would later say, explaining why he walked out anyway, leaving some money with the charge nurse. She pressed the notes into your mother's hand, unable to look her in the eye.

So you had a father in the form of a name registered on your birth certificate. A father who lived wildly in your childhood imagination, a debonair hero in a smart suit and tie, a man who was capable of the most amazing feats. A doctor, you thought, or a scientist, a man who couldn't be with you because he was needed elsewhere, needed the same way that comic book heroes were needed; the kind of man who had a mission instead of a family. "The Amazing Invisible Bastard," your mother once called him, knowing that you idolized him so, but she apologized immediately, her hands pruney from the dishwater as she lifted your chin up towards her face.

Your mother had a photograph of him, taken by his parents on holiday near Southampton. In the photo he is sixteen, wearing dark trousers rolled up above his knees, a shirt with thin vertical stripes. Bent over at the waist, he's reaching into the water about a foot from shore. Someone must have called "Henry" just then because he's looking up towards the camera with the kind of smile that isn't prepared. "Still looked like that at twenty," Mum would say, closing the roll-top desk where she kept the photo. There was a litany: "Henry William of the Westcotts of Kensington, blue eyes, Eton educated, father a barrister, mother liked to garden. Summer home at Southampton." And on it went for two minutes or so depending on how many questions you asked, or how many times the photograph had been taken out of the desk that month. You imagine now she thought it was her duty: salt in the wound every time the photograph was pulled off its shelf, every time her daughter took her back to the day Henry Westcott walked out on her. She said "Southampton," she described the rolling green lawn that led up to their doorstep; she said things like, "there were courts on the grounds, they liked to play tennis." But really she was thinking about Mercy General, how she woke up between the starched sheets of her hospital bed to see him standing there, how he walked out of her hospital room without speaking, turning around briefly in the light of the ward door.

The boy bending over in the water was all you ever had by way of a father, and even that didn't last long. By the time you were six the photo was gone.

"People fail inevitably, no matter how successful they seem," your mother said. That was her consolation for becoming a mother at twenty, for never finishing her nursing cert, for never falling in love. "People fail," she'd say, "as I have failed, as we all fail. And our consolation is this." *This* was always a gesture to something solid—the flowers blooming in the back garden, the picture of Gran and Grandpa on the settee, the wobbly old kitchen table with dinner just set out. So you prepared yourself for failure, found it every day in school work and at the play-ground and in tromping through the sitting room with your boots on. But for all your family's failed efforts, at least you had a home where you could stand in the doorway, growisng up, drawing conclusions about the world without getting rained on. And even that—rain falling onto the porch from the gutters—was a lesson in daring and proximity. "Emma," your mother would snap, "get in here before you catch your death!" But you didn't listen to her. And running through rain gutters was only your first step.

Two rooms in the back of your grandmother's house—this is where you grew up. The wallpaper in the bedroom was a faded yellow with cream flowers traced in brown. There was one double bed in the corner and your small desk was wedged against the other wall. You had this, plus a sitting room where you took your meals; it was painted baby blue after you first moved in.

On the best days, sunshine came in through the bedroom windows, the shutters opened to the garden. You played games under your mum's supervision as she sat on the back steps drinking tea. "She's growing up," you remember hearing your Gran say; she was looking out at you from the open window.

"A fine girl for all her wicked ways," your mother replied, watching you kick the neighbour's football against the back fence.

"Still, Elizabeth, she could use some direction."

"And what is it you think I have to give her?"

Order

"Women crave order," your mother confessed. And she did not mean the order implied by well-cornered bedsheets, flawless tax returns or curt architecture. No, we do not crave the well-marked master plan of gallant men, complete with flags and sweeping tales about the nobility of control. Women, she said, crave the order of place. *Here is my rage, there is my pain, over in this corner you'll find two days of labour, and in this place, just here, beside my left eye, you'll find passion.* And we stand in these places, on the doorsteps of our London homes, knocking our heads against walls one minute and ploughing them furtively through clouds the next. We rest our heads in our hands and we wait for an explosion that never arrives. "It is 1972," your mother would say, "batten down the hatches—anything is possible!" And off she'd go to Croften's Quick Stitch, making her hands busy, sewing hems and inlines, waiting with the rest of us for her day to come. But we swept the doorstep for nothing, you think; we planted the garden in incorrigible rows.

Now we live with our appointments, our calendars, needles and threads. We live with what little order we had before the world conspired to take it away. Perhaps your mother remembers waking up alone on July mornings, too sure of summer, lying under the sheets counting fingers and toes—five, yes, five. Smiling at the perfection of them until there were more fingers and toes to count than her own, more to do with her hands than interlace them with the hands of a lanky blond-haired boy on the shore in Southampton.

You learned anatomy in secondary school, the finer points, could recite the major muscle groups in ascending order. You scribbled and passed notes in class when the specifics of reproduction were addressed. At home you mastered cross-stitching and needlepoint. What else was there to know? You could already ride a bike fairly well in traffic and could greet everyone in the neighbourhood by name. And you were not alone in your delusion; your mother also believed these things would prepare you, that grammar and geometry might somehow be enough. So she stayed in the bedroom and read in the wingback chair, keeping her eye on you to make sure you were studying.

And there were chores.

"Emma, be a dear and wash up, will you?"

"Of course, Mum."

"Emma, could you run to the shoppe for butter," for beans, for bread ... what have you. The reiteration of "Emma would you wash," "Emma could you—" made each task familiar, more the same. Your mother wanted as much order as two rooms in a London house could afford. She wanted your adolescence to pass in controlled increments of supervised time. Because of her devotion to order, you never took trips; you even missed the class excursion to the museum because Mum diagnosed you with the flu. Rarely were you out of her reach. There were no sleepovers and no parties at the house. "Order," is what your mother called it, but to you Order was a monster who slept in the doorway, howling voraciously at anyone trying to get in or out of the house. Your mother fed him regularly and so why should he go anywhere else? "Set a place for Order at the table and for God's sake give him his elbow room." Order, you later realized, was no ordinary house guest, he was the great conspiracy of your childhood, the strap across your knuckles for unruly behaviour during history class, the bell ending your day at school, the clock on the sitting room wall measuring the ten minutes it should take you to get home. Order refused to let you kiss Michael Dunne in the closet at Shelly Emmet's party, even though there were only the two of you in amongst the boots and rain slickers.

"Come on, Emma, kiss me."
  "I can't."
  "It was a fair spin! You have to."
  "Shut-up, Michael. I just can't."

Order smugly walking you home that night at nine P.M., just as you were told, Order tucking you into bed an hour and a half later with a quick kiss to the forehead. Order asleep in the house, his luggage unpacked for good.

Stations

We do not want what our mothers have taken for themselves. Usually it is not enough, often it is simply wrong. In Crofton's Quick Stitch at closing time you meet your mother and walk from her shop, past the lock, down to Sainsbury's. Fussing over the price of greens, she sorts through them with both hands trying to find some worth buying. Suddenly she has become her own mother, realizing this only when she makes the cashier wait for the exact change, her hand scraping along the bottom of her black satchel. She stops. Everyone is watching her. The frumpy peroxided woman next in line smiles encouragingly—"Go on, dear"—but there is no moving forward from this. "Mum," you nudge her gently with your elbow and she turns, blankly. "Mum." You hand the cashier a ten-pound note from your cardigan pocket, gather up the grocery bags and usher your mother out past the magazine rack into the busy entryway and beyond into the parking lot.

Her face is in her hands, her whole body shuddering. Cars pull in and out all around you. A green Vauxhall backs indelicately into the space next to where you're standing. Now would be the time, you think, to gather our wits and meagre savings and skip out into the country. Now would be the time to holiday up in the Lake District rather than let her sit through another summer of grandmother's diatribes and the *Daily Sun*. You smile reassuringly at the driver of the Vauxhall. "She's all right," you say, but you're thinking, *this is it, the last straw.* You imagine your mother mentally summing up the family history in the check-out lane, the lot of it finally getting to her: you, your belly bulging out from under your jacket, repeating all her mistakes as if you admired them. And she can't even chastise you, can only root around in her bag for the five pounds and thirty-two pence she owes, saying "Just a minute now, just a minute," the same way her mother has always done.

We are stuck, you think, we are in need of rescue. But there is no life raft, no weekend in the country, no holiday down the road; there is only a middle-aged man stepping out of a Vauxhall, a man who nods, closes his car door and walks away.

Standing there in the parking lot, you think of her with him, the boy who would become your father. You remember her yellow sleeveless summer dress and tiny pearl necklace. In your imagination they are away from the beach at a small wood fire, her hands over her mouth because he has just made her laugh. Wild infallible happiness and all that it leads to. Sometimes we know there is no such thing as choice, only what-it-is-that-happens and the irony of retrospect. It was that way with Adam, although you saw him coming long before he arrived.

"Let this be a lesson to you," your mother screamed one morning when you were sixteen. She was standing over a sink full of dishes, a deep arced cut on her index finger. "Never lift your skirt for anyone." But we all do, in time. You couldn't tell her then that you knew it was inevitable, that you longed for it. Instead you pulled out the tiny sliver of glass, ran her hand under a cold stream of water.

We are our mother's children. There are times, even now, when you feel your face set in a certain expression and you know you've seen exactly that look on your mother's face a thousand times. But you don't want to become her. You don't want the empty bed, the underpaid work, the weight of the past hanging on you like chains. This is why Adam matters, though you try to tell yourself otherwise. This is why tonight you'll go back to your flat in Camden and try to call him, to patch things up.

In the parking lot your mother is wringing her hands, the groceries on the asphalt between you. The vegetables are starting to wilt in the sun.

"Mum?"

She nods in your direction, wipes her eyes one last time then pushes her fingers against her eyelids.

"All right?"

She sucks in her breath, exhales, then straightens up, smiling as though she's as composed as the Queen. You half expect her to look around the parking lot, to lift her arm, turn her wrists and wave.

"Shall we?" she says after a minute, bending down then starting off, two of the grocery bags in hand. You pick up the other bag and walk alongside her, placing the small of your palm in the centre of her back, the two of you together making your way along Jasper Street.

To Let

The front window of the flat was obscured by the large sign that hung from an iron-rail balcony on the floor above:

Gray, Young and Co.

Camden Flat To Let

You had finished bringing in the last box and remember standing outside with your mother, summing it up.

"Great neighbourhood, Mum."

"Not really."

"Yes Mum, really."

"A mess on the weekend, Emma. Markets bring out the hoodlums."

"But the rent is great."

"Mice, probably."

But she had put her hand up to your cheek and smiled, adding, "That dress suits you, dear." What was there left to say? You had both looked up at the window, your mother had cleared her throat. It reminded you of the day you went off to stay at Aunt Clara's for the week. You were eight and full of the newness of things. Your mother said she needed a rest and at any rate, Clara should spend more time with her niece. "God knows," your mother said, "her house is big enough." So you got a ticket south to Salisbury, memorized how many stops, the names of towns in between. Clara would take the train down with you but you'd come back alone. Even though it had all been rehearsed your mother had a hard time of it, hanging onto your hand until Clara pried it from her, saying "Liz, Liz it'll be all right, give her over now, it's just the week."

"It'll be all right Mum," you said it then at eight, and you said it again ten years later, on the day you took the flat, the Camden Street noise picking up around you. Although you knew it wasn't going to be just the week this time, it was the beginning of your lives apart. You'd squeezed her hand then let it go. With that she'd stepped away, closing the trunk of the rented car and making ready to leave. "Call if you need," she'd said too cheerfully, ducking into the driver's seat, starting the ignition. You wouldn't need to call her but knew you'd do it anyway, ask for a hand to do the cleaning or if you might come by for dinner. Then, thinking that she might be expecting a wave, you'd flailed your arm in a dramatic gesture while she drove off down the street, grinding the gearshift, nearly crossing into the other lane before going over the bridge.

The noise from the market that first Saturday had you out of bed at seven. People shouting and even the rattle of vending stands going up carried the two blocks to your window. You'd tossed your robe over the rail in the closet and made for the boxes marked "Clothes." Having amassed some savings from summer employ cashiering at the Quick Stitch, you'd considered going out to buy something to improve the decor but then you'd figured out that the cost of fabric for curtains, new cutlery and plates, and a proper bed frame, would do you in. So you'd decided not to go overboard, having only optimism to carry you. You were eighteen. There was a phone on the floor in the bedroom, and a mattress. You had canned food and cookware, books and an old radio; beyond that, you were starting anew. You'd dressed in black trousers and a blue long-sleeved shirt, admired yourself in the mirror that hung inside the closet. *This is your flat,* you remember thinking, *you are finally out on your own.*

Outside you had thrashed through the market with what seemed like half the population of London. *One pound ten for the best scone in the city,* said the sign in the bakery window. One pound ten—exorbitant, but you bought the scone anyway, and on that morning, with the hussle and chaos of the market going up around you, it was indeed the best.

Browning's Book Sellers

"Books bought as often as they are sold.
Browning's Book Sellers, specializing in first editions, art,
architecture and maps. If you have an original or collectible,
we want it."

WILL PAY A

FAIR PRICE

"Will Pay A Fair Price," the motto of sorts, was written in brisk script on a square board that hung over the walnut bookshelves. You remember it from your first day browsing, how you wished you had something valuable enough to sell. Here were wall-to-wall handbound leather volumes with gilded edgings, here was the currency of learning; they made your paperback Dover Classics seem dim. In the middle of the room there was a small Edwardian desk that held a brass lamp and clackity old cash register. In the far corner, rolled maps leaned against bookshelves like stoic ambassadors surveying the room. The simplicity of the shop impressed you, as did Mr. Browning in his bowler and smart black suit and tie. He nodded your way when you first came in, the paunch of his chin bobbing up and down over his collar. When he saw you take a book on Gavin Hamilton off the shelf he nodded again, asked if you had an art background. "Museums," you said, still browsing.

The next time you went into the shop, Browning asked how much you knew about Charles Rennie Mackintosh; he was looking over a new book. So you told him what little you knew, mentioning an exhibit at the Tate. Browning responded with a diatribe on Scottish art, followed by a well-articulated lesson on the history of bookselling. He seemed happy to have a customer so interested in what he had to say. Then he pulled some books out of a corner cabinet, showing you, among other things, an early 18th-century missal. The two of you chatted about an unconventional illustration of Mary until someone came in to inquire about a book they wanted to sell.

When Browning mentioned he was looking for help you'd decided to apply. Maybe your CV was thin, but in the year since moving you'd made up for all the museum trips you'd missed as a child, and that, as well as your enthusiasm, might be qualification enough in his opinion. Besides, the Quick Stitch could be slow and you were always the one who was sent home when only a few people were needed.

"There is nothing better than an old book," Browning had exclaimed the first week you worked there. And you believed it; his happiness was contagious. He loved books and his love for them gave him a youthful quality, a glee you admired. Often he would shoot up mid-conversation, saying, "Did I mention the Caxton, Ms. Langford?" or "Why I recall ..." and on he would go, hands gesturing towards the walls or touching the spine of a specific book. Here, you'd thought, is something to learn about, here is a learned man. So you'd worked with Browning daily as he showed you the ropes, encouraging his tales despite his fanaticism. But that, you reckoned, is love—a sort of fanaticism, something that can't be contained at all.

Arrivals

And that has somehow led you here, as if moments can be traced from one decisive point to the next: Birth, bicycle accident, senior dance with Charlie Benson, move to Camden Town, buying Winston at the market, employ at Browning's, followed by Adam, and now the seemingly inevitable, impending return to birth.

Your Aunt Clara, up for the weekend to visit, plays at numerology. Over lunch at Chin Lo's you tell her about Adam's reaction to the baby, so she takes out a calculator and some twenty numbers later she comes up with "eight," which means water, because it is always water with her. After finishing her eggroll, she informs you that a sideways eight represents infinity and a race track with sharp turns and no straightaways. "Inevitable," she sighs, "inevitable," as if everything was always headed for eight and the twenty most important events in your lifetime were just wee fractions of the eight that now rules your life with what little glory is left. "Greece," she sighs while picking up the tab, "you should have waylaid for Greece."

She walks you back to Camden and comes round to the core of her advice. "Leave him out of it," she says, "he obviously isn't worth it. Raise the baby alone."

"So Greece," you say, wanting to avoid the topic of Adam and giving in to the idea of a blue-on-blue watery landscape, the whitewash of houses in the fat round sun. Bambina? Bambino? You can't think of how to say baby, you can't name a city in Greece save Athens. You have, at best, seen a travel advert or two, maybe a film set on one of the Islands. The images in your head may come from books. Hard to say. Still, an inviting idea. Greece. You furrow your brow. Clara watches you, explains, "An analogy, Pet," as if she were a mindreader. And then, as if she's finally fed up with you, she starts into it: her ideology on the single life, how nothing beats it and how a woman can have her own success only when she stops obliging men. "They get in the way of it, of everything." She flips her poppy-print scarf over her shoulder, pulls her cigarettes out of her purse and picks up the pace. "Look at your mother, your grandmother, look at yourself." You try to catch up with her, but she is dizzying— lighting her cigarette, flipping her hair over her shoulder, making blanket proclamations all in the same long stride.

Truth be told you'd rather be in Greece belly-up to the sun like a pale beached whale than hauling yourself along after Clara, your due date closing in. Too bad it's all become so pointed. Too bad she didn't really mean what she'd said about Greece. There is nothing more appealing than the prospect of escape. You can easily imagine an even bronze tan, olive trees and fresh-squeezed fruit juices, the baby playing on the beach. You had even momentarily hoped that she was going to offer to spring for a one-way ticket overseas. Greece, water, a sideways eight.

"Raise the baby alone," Clara had said, staring at you as you rounded the corner to your flat. Adding "Look at the lot of us," delivered with no small measure of exasperation, although you still can't decide if she meant your family or your gender. History's sleight of hand getting the better of us once again.

Returning to the Question

Your doctor rubs the ultrasound paddle over your stomach and on the monitor you see a watery figure on its back, head in profile. For the first time this is real; the baby is born to you in this moment, is no longer a series of aches and jabs or an unseemly burden that has you holding banisters with one hand and your back with the other. Now the baby has become something living outside of you, each blip of the heart monitored and amplified out into the room. *A boy*, you think, although from his position you can't tell. *A boy,* as if intuition could make it so. *And how beautiful the perfection of his little hands.*

This is the first photograph you will have of him, not like the other ultrasounds where he's all minnowy and oddly postured; no, this is the baby close to birth, this is a child sleeping. When you get back to the flat you place the ultrasound under a pineapple magnet on the fridge, decide you'll photocopy it for Mum and Clara to see. You think about handing out copies to strangers on the street but the cost is prohibitive and you know the magic of it would be lost on them. It's the simple, timely miracles that capture people's interest—the market popping up out of nowhere on weekends; the stretch of the sun reflecting on the Canal; scones fresh from the bakery in Chalk Farm. The average passerby has no room for anyone's miracle save her own.

But if not for miracles, what is it you have to give him, small as he is? What gestures, what fullness of life and what knowledge of the world? There is the bookstore you work in with its yellowing pages and beautiful art, there is the park off Old Street with its animal-shaped shrubbery and buoyant flowers. The rhubarb crumble recipe your grandmother passed on to your mother and she to you. Winston with his tail-wagging enthusiasm. And then there are the walls of the baby's room, which need repainting, the crib from the market with its missing rails, and the promise of baby clothes in your grandmother's attic, although you've no sewing machine of your own to mend them with. How is it that the world can narrow enough for children to be born when so much needs doing? Every day, women bring babies into the world between work and the afternoon meal. They pause in birthing pools and then run back into their lives as if they'd had a mere swim. They jump back into their routines, their BMWs, their work, a baby under one arm, heading straight to their husband or lover, and off the three of them speed into the whirl of it all, scarves flapping madly in the wind. Mother couldn't walk for that first week and the days went by like seasons. She thought you'd be three years old by the time she could sit and rock you on her knee. How will you manage when it's common for the flu to put you under for days at a time, so that you can barely make it from bed to let the dog out in the morning? The struggle is too wide. Practised breathing only gets you through the very first part. After that it's taxis and traffic jams, dirty diapers, rashes and the stitches still healing.

The ultrasound is on the fridge in the centre of the kitchen, in the middle of a row of houses in Camden Town in England, and somewhere out there Adam is traipsing around with Victoria on a business holiday. "Going out to the country," he'd said when you'd phoned the office Monday morning. "But I'll be back on Thursday. We could meet then."

"That'd be great, Adam."

"Where?"

"The Old Stand?"

"Done. And Emma?"

"Yep?"

"I'm sorry about what happened, about what I said. It was all—"

And when he can't find the right way to say it, you say it for him. "A bit of a surprise?"

Adam is with Victoria and the two of them are probably out for dinner at this moment, ringing up exotic appetizers on the company charge card and becoming witty and flirtatious with wine. Not you. You are bending over the dog's bowl picking up the stray kibbles on the floor while waiting for your beans to warm in the pot. It's enough to make you lose your mind were you not the better, or were it not for that tiny hand with its upward gesture, bringing your eyes back to the fridge. *Hello there*, you smile, staring at the picture, until the smell of burning beans brings you round.

The Old Stand

Thursday afternoon Adam meets you for lunch at The Old Stand as promised, and in spite of yourself you are sitting in the familiar snug, knees touching every so often under the table, hands wrapped around pint glasses, your finger circling the rim. This is proof it has happened, this is a replay lest we forget. The oak benches with their tacked leather backing are not a sign of Eden, only of this specific hovel around the bend from Leicester Square where deceit comes in its only form—pint of Samuel Smith, flushed cheeks, resurrection of old wants. He is here to inquire, do his service, be a good soldier. He is here because without the baby and his unanswered phone calls in those first months you might still be lovers, you might still be in love.

"I think I might leave her, really."

"Liar."

"Emma, really."

You open your mouth to protest but swallow the bait nonetheless, a current of brown ale washing it down. Close your mouth and swallow again; he might leave her. But he won't. Maybe they had a bad business trip, an argument in the lounge of the hotel. When there's a bump in the road Adam always waylays, says it's time to pull over. But you can no more see him hitchhiking from the roundabout than you can see him telling Victoria to open the door and get out. Surely it was one argument in the hotel, people milling around the marble columns and check-in counter craning to hear. Maybe she let fly an accusation. And that was enough to shake him, for the moment anyway.

"I was going to call you." He says this to sound attentive, he says this to make up for being an idiot, for not knowing how these things are done. You can tell that right now he is trying in his own way to please you. This is how it started—that adoration, that singular, attentive, unblinking look.

"I don't even know why we're here." You say it but you're lying. It took eight months and one week to get to this. Three months of not returning his calls before he stopped ringing. Two months of replaying his voice on the machine, rewinding those messages so many times you thought the tape would break. "Emma, why aren't you calling?" "Em, are you there?" And it took three months to work up the nerve to go see him, to convince yourself enough time had passed, that you really wouldn't care.

"Have you chosen a name yet?" he asks, his thumb moving in circles on the inside of your wrist.

After an hour you turn the conversation back to bank accounts and deposit dates, you hand him a copy of the bank book, a number to call in case there should be a delay. This is business after all; this, you want to believe, is why you asked him to come. Adam takes the bank book and looks at it, he runs his hand across his forehead, squints, and settles back into the bench. "The firm is doing well but it'll be hard to keep Victoria from noticing." He tells you he might pretend he's investing in a new building, or maybe he won't say anything at all. You smooth his tousled hair, brown strands sticking out between your fingers, and hope for the best. He takes your hand and puts his lips on your wrist.

"I wish I wanted this baby, Em."

You are up and out the door so quickly you don't have time

to think of what might have been left on the table, what was left unsaid. Checking for the keys to the flat you click your handbag closed and hurry down the street into the sharp afternoon air. What had you dared to hope for? Where was your reserve? Your own questions are now answered. Questions you had never dared to ask aloud. What if your mother had tried to contact your father? What if she had written, gone to Southampton, pounded on the door? What if she had retraced her steps, met him on the beach where everything was born, what if she'd snapped photos and sent them to him as reminders? Nothing. Nothing would have changed. A father cannot be made out of air and wishing, and the modern age has brought us no spells.

Inventory

Two travelling trunks filled with worn dresses from the fifties.

Cardboard box of your baby clothes.

School annuals, stuffed toys and Clara's collection of horse figurines.

Grandpa's favourite tweed cap in a hat box from Squires.

That is only the beginning. Five feet into Grandma's attic and already you have to restack boxes, rehang clothes bags, just to push along on your makeshift pathway. Ten minutes into it and already you're out of breath.

"Towards the back righthand corner," Grandma calls up from the hallway below. "Under the box with the tea towels your mother sent from Scotland."

The bickering starts somewhere below you.

"Never liked those, did you, Mum?"

"No, sweetheart, I didn't. All in the gesture though."

A shoe rack filled with Granddad's shoes, still perfectly polished.

Volumes of *Encyclopedia Britannica* from the sixties.

Odd assortment of lamp shades piled one atop the other, culminating in a pea green tasselled number that triggers vague recollections.

Under a box marked "Tea Towels" there's a sewing box without a speck of dust on it.

"Found it, Gran."

That woman may have a bit of trouble getting around these days but her ability to pack it all in is certainly not in question.

Heading back out you shuffle along, a few inches at a time, on your bum. You pull the sewing machine along beside you.

"Need help?" your Gran calls from somewhere in the house below you. And you roll your eyes while answering "No." Three feet closer to the attic door you stop to catch your breath. Next to your left knee you notice an old football with unravelled seams. Above you, four gaudy picture frames are fastened to the rafters with string; there are even more of them along the slope of the east wall. Beside them, more stacks of boxes marked "Clara—winter", "Clara—summer," "Misc. gloves, etc.", "Board games" and "Utensils."

To your right there are stacks of record albums in old crates. Mostly the London Philharmonic, and a few Sinatra, the odd collection of show tunes.

And closer to the door you find an old Agfa camera, its instruction manual and warranty organized in their plastics.

You drag the sewing machine, camera and your own round baggage along with you and head for the dust-filled square of natural light beyond the boxes. You consider yelling down for help. Instead you make your way towards the door in manageable increments, stopping every now and again to marvel at what's been accumulated. Empty old snuff tins tied in a clear plastic bag. As if your Gran had spent her life picking up after Granddad, afraid to let any of it fall by the way. His kind of cancer giving her enough time to organize and inventory reminders until an entire museum was established, people coming ready with their tickets while its subject was still alive. The winter he died your mother was nineteen and just starting her certificate in nursing. She's told you she'd come home and bathe him after classes, change his bedding, rolling him towards her as she'd been shown, how he just lay there as if anything he could say was an admission towards dying. Your mum says he was a good man and your Gran doesn't say much at all. You open up the bag of snuff tins and imagine the smell of him, remember the way he looked in the photos taken the year before he died.

Towards the front of the attic you come across hot water bottles and electric hot pads, all stacked in plastic and packed away. There's a box marked "William—flannel pyjamas." A box marked "Emma—toys," which you decide to come back for later. Better that than make the rounds at other people's rummage sales or brave the boot sales at the far end of the market. Wedging yourself the last two feet towards the attic opening you feel a pang, as if the baby has shifted inside of you, as if he, too, is crowded and looking for elbow room. You put your hand against the bulk of your stomach and press down with your palm, then you shimmy towards the attic door, your skirt spreading out over the thin pile carpet so that you can feel the bristly strands scratching the backs of your legs. The baby has stopped moving. You sit and wait to feel some kind of movement again but nothing comes. Now you're not sure which is worse—the cartwheel, the somersault, his exuberant demonstration of womb gymnastics or the hush that follows, as if he's not really there at all.

This is when you realize that there is nothing here, nothing to show where you've come from. You look around the attic. Three generations as if they came from naught. You, your mother, Gran and the museum that makes up Gramps. And then nothing—not a hat box, not a handkerchief, not an old letter, naught. As if your family fell out of the blue, crawled out of the sea and onto this island. But babies are made and born, people make them, women give birth to them and are irrevocably changed. Where, you wonder, did your Gran come from, what man, what woman gave her her thin wrists, the high arch of her brows, her sloping shoulders, her name?

You dangle your foot down and touch the top step of the wood ladder. In the kitchen the women are arguing about the tea towels again. Winston is wagging his tail, looking up at you from the floor below. "Coming down!" you say, trying to enlist some help. "Pregnant woman on the move!" One foot firmly on the top rung. Your mum and Gran coming out to help you down. Slowly, you think, you're getting there. One foot and then the next.

A Sort of Alimony

Adam gives you snapdragons, your favourite flower, which you set, wrapped, on the kitchen table while he wipes his feet on the mat. It's two weeks to the delivery date and after he cajoled you into it, after he called the flat three times and then dropped by the bookstore, after he pursued you like he'd done before, apologizing for things he'd never even done, you said yes, come over, but only to get this business out of the way. You want it to be over, to get back to the matter at hand; but for now this is the matter, and the sight of him in your door frame melts your resolve and makes you dizzy.

We would picnic in Hyde Park, you'll tell the baby. *We made love in the Portobello studio his friend had rented, we ate croissants he brought from the bakery. There is a scar that stretches from his hip to his navel. Here are the books we read, the only film we ever saw together was out in Bath at the matinee, a romance, the title I can't remember. And he came one afternoon to the flat in Camden Town right before you were born and he placed his hand across my belly like this to say hello to you. There were flowers too. He was tall, filling up the entryway. He placed his hand here, and he left.*

But first he drinks the tea you offer him and settles into the worn wingback in the corner of the sitting room. He confesses that he has no idea how to go about this. He spreads his hands out in a gesture of surrender, he shrugs and lets his hands fall back into his lap. You point out that he negotiated the affair component of your relationship well enough. That more often than not, he came through when he said he'd be there. "But that was different, Em. This isn't just between us."

You bring out your grandmother's Agfa and sitting on the floor in front of him click a few pictures to develop and save for future questions. They say you should gather health histories and genealogies; institutions have done studies on children who are adopted or orphaned, have developed preventative measures—"information," they say—to stave off the black hole of the unknown.

*He likes Indian food from a restaurant called The Himalaya—*you'd start with telling the baby the hospitable bits—*he wears collared shirts and thinly striped ties. He can't hold a tune, is ticklish about the hips. His wedding band is thick and gold with a small inset diamond you can barely see. He goes to football games with his son who has fair hair like his mother. The boy's name is Justin. I saw him play one afternoon at Hastings School, he was quite good. There is a little girl, they called her Virginia. Your father's office is filled with brown leather and glass tables with brass legs; there are pictures of the family on his desk.*

"I might love you more if you weren't so difficult." You're lying on the floor while Adam massages your foot from the armchair. Winston, stretched out beside you, twitches in his sleep.

"Not difficult," you reply, and even though you are tired of playing emotional tag, you smile because he does love you and at this moment the idea of it is almost enough.

"Yes, Emma," more pressure on the instep, "quite difficult."

"Then why do you keep coming 'round?"

"Smitten, I suppose," and he kisses the tip of your toe. Everything is an adolescent game with him, as if you had nothing better to do with your time than to run wide circles around him. *You're it, Adam!* You imagine a field full of children play-ing tag, their faces puckered and eyes squinched tight to the sun. *You're it.* And you can see him there, Adam shouting "Come and get me," the way you did so exuberantly when the game was played in school. *And so,* you think, *why don't you start running,* although you're half hoping Adam will catch *you* and not the other way around.

Adam releases your right foot and you place the other one in his lap. He starts kneading the arch with his thumbs but you can see he's looking at the bulk of your pregnancy, looking at it with a mixture of awe and fear.

Lines

After Adam leaves, you go to the kitchen and rinse his cup, wondering why he came round to Browning's Bookstore, why he insisted he had to see you. It's the same old routine without all the old desperation: he wants to be with you but inevitably falls short of the mark. "You can't please everyone." It's your mother who's fond of saying this. And maybe she's right, maybe half of something is better than nothing at all.

The radio is on in the sitting room and you can hear talk of mitochondrial DNA on the BBC. They've done a special report on the newly discovered skeletons in Africa. There's a genetic code, they say, one that remains intact, one that's passed on by women, generation to generation; a distaff history all the way from Lucy to you. You imagine it as a sort of helix, spinning about in the bloodstream, a whirling dervish minus the fez. An in-the-beginning-was-the-helix kind of scenario; or maybe it's a map, a plan, a connect-the-dots sketch that leads back to your matrilineal home.

"Mitochondria," the announcer says, "is from the Greek for thread." It's a language, you think, this genetic marker, this sign post, this hand-me-down. Your ancestors' genome transferred into numbers and then letters, your strain in the whole of evolution becoming broad arithmetic and then words. The words becoming paragraphs, a litany that could be passed on from one woman to the next like a favourite skirt. A litany that begins with "The weather is frightful: too much bloody dirt, dust and wind. The last sign of life we saw in this desert was the backs of the men heading south for food. We've given up on them and are off in search of fresh water, the fabled tropics et cetera et cetera."

And then the disappointment of Eden once they arrived: cold coastal winds, hard soil, the paunch of bogs and valleys. Sea springing up on all sides. The failed explorers finally making their way home, admitting that north might have been the way to go all along. Still, all things considered, they dug in their heels and stayed. And the men fell in line. And the women had children. Years passed. The continents split and shifted. And then, one sunny afternoon, Adam showed up with the apple. "You should have known better," your ancestors would say. And maybe they were right. But you took the fruit anyway.

After you first met Adam in the arboretum at the London Zoo, his children probably off at the tiger cages with his wife ... after you dropped your strawberry ice-cream on the toe of his shiny black shoe, introducing yourself while laughing ... after going down on one knee, napkin in hand ... there was botanical small talk, and inquiries were made. Numbers were exchanged and written on scraps of paper—his on your grocery list, yours on a ticket for the carousel. Was it then that the numbers were recorded in the DNA diary, alongside your mother's indiscretion and your grandmother's rigid traditions? Does all this information make its way through your skin and then into the bloodstream and through the gene wall? You imagine all the trivial bits of information that are recorded and then the one bit that matters, as if you'd won the Lotto. You imagine the sound of cymbals and horns: "This is the number to memorize, this is the one": 450-1832 on a grocery list, a witty man's handwritten scrawl encoded forever, when the price of bananas and oranges would have served you better and done less harm.

Resuscitation

Adam is not the monster you make him out to be. At least he's coming around to visit. When he was at the flat a few days ago, he asked if he could come back. So against your better judgment you stand in front of the bathroom mirror, preening. Every pore of your being tells you you love him, in whatever odd and maligned shape that love has taken. As expected, he lied to his wife those first few weeks about where he was going, and he didn't tell you he was married until it was too late. The next two months consisted of a series of arrangements and plans followed by a number of cancellations. He confessed one night that he didn't want to get caught. But forfeiting discretion he racked up restaurant bills on his credit card, went home with wrinkled shirts to immediate showers. This leads you to believe, his record notwithstanding, that he has always been in possession of a most singular kind of honesty. That, and a poxy haircut that falls over his right eye when not slicked back for work.

It is that same infuriatingly rigid honesty—an honesty he shares mostly with you, along with his stubbled chin and penchant for Chaplin films, airing most often at three A.M.—that you miss. He'd telephone you: "Charlie's on!" And good god if you ever really cared, but you turned on the telly just the same, as if it was close enough to being with him. Honesty: he tells you he doesn't want the baby. A shabby sense of honour: he tells you he will leave his wife. Honesty again: that he tried but can't. That he wants you regardless, will buy you a gold collar studded with diamonds if you'll wear it and accept that it might be all he can give you in the end. Adam is not to blame that you said yes, that you closed your eyes and hoped for more.

The first sign of trouble came a year ago, on the way back to London from a weekend in Bath. Adam had been meeting a client who wanted to commission a plan for redesigning an old character home into offices. You'd busied yourself that morning in the shops and later, bored, sat along the Avon, throwing grass into the river, reed by reed. You thought you might wade in for a bit, strip down to your knickers and thinning wool jumper, but you were too lazy to bother with the wet of it all, and in truth, you are not the best wader. Why take your chances in even the shallowest water pool when there's no one round to rescue you? That weekend, the weather was perfectly mild and the after-noons were long, the woman who owned the bed-and-breakfast on Holyrod Lane singing TuRaLuLaRuLa in the kitchen while peeling potatoes, an apron over her lilac dress. You were mak-ing love every hour or so up in the low-ceilinged bedroom, the mattress springs squeaking every time you moved. The woman's singing grew louder as if trying to drown out the sound. You remember the mischievous look in Adam's eyes, his mouth mov-ing across your breast.

At the tube station in Acton you got out of the car so no one in town would see you. Your coat had been stuck in the door all the way from Bath, the corner of it was muddy and wet.

"I can't see you next week. Victoria's family is in town from Bristol."

"When are they leaving?"

"Sunday."

"Sunday then?" and you hated yourself for saying it.

"It might be too soon. I'll ring."

And he left you there having made no commitment whatsoever, without even the slightest bit of guilt. So you stood there and seethed, watching the back of the BMW as he made his way towards Bayswater, the red of the car's dirty tail lights flashing on, then off.

It's just past six and you hear the sound of an engine being shut off in the street below and once again it is Adam, here at his appointed and convenient time. Winston makes for the door, giving a low growl at the sound of footsteps coming up the stairway. You've made of yourself what you can, although no item of clothing feels flattering these days and much depends on the extent of your preoccupation. You're lucky if you remember to comb your hair. You tug at Winston's collar so that he backs up enough to let you crack open the door. If Adam comes up the hallway with two maniacal heads, his hands stretched out zombie-like in front of him, if he has electrodes embedded in his skull, then you were wrong and he is a diabolical monster. If he comes with flowers or his lopsided grin, or even if he simply arrives, then perhaps he is redeemable, maybe even some kind of saint.

The Houses We Build

Your mother in her late middle age has turned to crafts. Her rooms are overflowing with painting kits and wood panels for the ornate birdhouses she wants to sell to The Sparkling Brook Nature Shop come summer. "And what of Adam?" she wonders, her hands busying themselves with carpenter's glue and two thin pieces of oak arched like gothic window frames. And you retell the story: the occasional engagements, like this afternoon at the newsstand, two o'clock sharp, the old feelings revisited along with the status of the baby's account—first deposit made.

"When you were two, maybe three, I had a fling, if that's what one calls it, with Tom who ran the newsstand down the way. Must be something romantic about a newsstand," she says, gluing the archway into place on the wooden base of a platform, a platform that will become a gothic cathedral for finches. Oddly enough, your mother's dalliance with a newsstand man doesn't surprise you; rather, you realize, it was always to be expected. People, by force of habit, search out whatever it is that might sustain them, and sometimes, you suppose, are appeased for a while. Your mother is just like the rest of us, and quite, in her way, like you. "It was the *Guardian* I'd buy. Weekdays." With that, she squeezes more Ready Glue out of the tube, affixing a buttress above the birdhouse entry.

"So, what of Adam?" she begins again, absentmindedly making conversation while she sands another buttress by hand.

"Adam is well. I've decided to keep seeing him."

"At the bookstore then?"

"At the flat."

"You're not—?"

"No, mother."

You could have this conversation with anyone. Victoria even, who only knows you as a supplier of expensive hardcovers—the Nash that Adam prefers and a *Guide to English Homesteads* which she purchased for him at Christmas. The Missus herself coming into Browning's to pick up a copy of *The Picturesque Cottage* for an anniversary present. "My husband Adam has your card." She dropped it onto the desk in front of you. Blonder and prettier than she was in the one photo you'd seen, and before you could clear your throat and recover she had sixty pounds out of her purse and was asking again for *The Picturesque Cottage*, clarifying, "My husband was going to pick it up; I thought I'd surprise him." But the book was at your flat on the bedside table and your explanations for misplacing it seemed inadequate. You could feel the flush of your cheeks.

"If you could find it, then, and I'll be back tomorrow."

"Of course." Standing up behind the desk and coming more than a few inches short of her, the shoulders of her cream linen jacket catching the light as she walked into the street.

The discussion is with your mother now, but she is preoccupied, so it might as well be anyone. Yes, even Victoria, on the doorstep of her Georgian home.

"And what of *The Picturesque Cottage*?" she'd inquire, "and what of Adam?"

"Adam is well. I've decided to keep seeing him."

"At the bookstore then?" She is confused, feels a bit muddled, wonders if you're still talking about books.

"No," you say, "at the flat."

"You're not—?" The idea occurs to her. An idea, followed by the gathering up of old suspicions, culminating suddenly in an understanding.

"No, Victoria, but we have and might do so again."

Your mother drops a buttress onto the floor and picks it up to find it covered with thin grey strands of carpet.

"Cripes." She uses a tea towel to clean it off and starts again with the carpenter's glue.

"Well. Do you love him?" she asks you, and not for the first time.

"Of course."

But you know this is a conversation you will not allow yourself to have with Victoria even though you had gone to Adam's doorstep daring it to happen. Even though you could have confessed that the cottages of Gloucestershire were open on your bedstand and that there was also a toothbrush, some boxers and a pressed white shirt she might care to lug home with her as well. You might have told her then that Adam was intending to take you on a driving tour of the cottages, you might have said he was thinking of leaving home. But too many people wailing about only creates confusion. And now, at this point and time, you are confused enough.

What does Victoria do beyond that doorway? Ready the children for school, heat scones and serve tea? Perform all her wifely duties with a reserved vigour that constrains her anger just enough? How many cups and saucers are thrown across the room only to be swept up minutes later? How tight-lipped can she be?

Perhaps you're breaking plate for plate, cup for saucer in

unison on opposite ends of the city. You restock at the market and she probably goes to Waterford's so he doesn't notice, never hears the crack of them over the door, his key already in the ignition.

The Flood

It has been raining in London for five days in a row. You must prepare yourself for what might happen. The baby is already one step ahead of the game, treading water in that other world, arms and feet flapping their one/two/stroke and breathe, one/two/stroke and breathe. You can feel him wake up in the morning for his first laps—seven A.M. in the kiddy pool. He is due in six days. The rain is still falling. The city is starting to flood. Like Aphrodite, he might be born from the sea, flung out between waves to coast on the thick foam that swallowed the country. Paintings of him will be made by future generations, the descendants of those who drove their power boats and yachts to the New World. Pictures will be drawn of the boy who rode the deluge to land, shells strung with seaweed hanging from his neck. And the perfection of him. He will be a god, a symbol of love, born not from indiscreet mortals who met on Thursdays in Leicester Square, but born from the heart of a raging current.

The wind changes direction and comes in swells against the bedroom window. Soon, you think, pulling the duvet over your shoulders, this whole building will groan and release itself to the current gathering in the street gutters below. And then off you will travel, the three of you—mother, baby, dog—all the houses in London disembarking to make way over the water. The baby will be born in the bedroom with Winston whining in the doorway. He'll grow up to see the world from your floating barge, geraniums on the sill the only thing he'll know of land. Call him Neptune and let Winston teach you both the dog paddle because you never took the time to learn to swim. Perhaps if the wind is blowing just so, and the fates favour you at all, you might come across a tire floating in the melee. With some skill and tied-together hosiery you might make the boy a swing in the door-way and on quieter nights he could rock himself into the house and out over the sea to know something of freedom. But you'll be alone. No one to guide you. The house at the mercy of the wind and currents, nothing to anchor you, no history you can haul aboard. There will just be the two of you trying to catch fish with chopsticks and earrings, the three of you waiting for the flood to end.

When you wake from this dream it is Tuesday and the rain has mostly abated. You roll over in the tangle of your sheets and put your hand on the mound of your belly, half surprised that you haven't given birth at all. Thankfully the house is solidly rooted and out the window you see a morning that's starting to clear. You wonder what it was you were missing in your dream. And where was Adam? He was probably sailing his old Georgian home to the nearest spit of land, he and Victoria were probably bailing.

The baby takes his fists and pounds out a morse code hello. You stare at your belly as if you might see it moving. In the dream the baby was a little man. A foot high and fully grown. He needed nothing. And there was nothing to give him. Brushing your teeth, you figure out what was missing in your dream. You resolve to ask your Gran about the family history. But first you get dressed for your check-up at the Camden Clinic. The swell is coming and any day your water might break.

Coming Round

You lean over as best you can in the bathtub while Adam dips
the sponge down into the water. Then he squeezes it along your
back. Your belly is huge and the baby was supposed to be due
next week but the doctor has put the date back by four or five
days.

"Victoria had awful pregnancies."

"That so?"

"Never let me see her naked past the fourth month."

"Not even to talk to the baby?"

"No, not really. I had to push my lips into the slits between
her buttonholes."

He runs the sponge down your back and along your hips.
You lean back against the wall of the tub and he makes soapy
circles around your stomach.

"She was miserable all through."

"Hmm, really?"

"It wasn't like this at all."

But you *are* starting to feel miserable. Yesterday you were at
Sainsbury's, cabbage and carrots in hand, crisscrossing the veg-
etable aisle from one end to the next. This, before noticing in the
mirror that your skirt was caught up in your tights, baring your
knickered behind for all of Camden Town to see. And that was
only the first of it. There was the nausea which stemmed more
from a headache than anything else, there was also a dull throbbing pain in your back, and more often than not these past few
weeks, there has been straight-out panic. I'm not ready, there's

too much to be done! Catch up on the Lamaze classes you missed, find the baby a father who can commit, run over the carpets with flea powder, gather presents for the child. It might have been the embarrassment at Sainsbury's—you even said hullo to Mr. Geary, the butcher—but it's also more than that. *Get it together, woman, you are not prepared. Gather your wits and seek out direction. Do something!* Rather than cry over indecision and Victoria's victory by ignorance, you clean like a demon, and after Adam leaves the house you clean again, starting with the room he occupied last.

The bathtub still full of soapy water, you stand on the damp mat wondering what will come of this confusion. You reach down and release the drain. Adam is being careful this time and it has not gone unnoticed. He comes by every other afternoon but only stays for an hour, going straight back to the office after lunch. He brings take-out, he pulls the mail out of the slot at the bottom of the steps, he fixes anything that's broken. But after watching the water spiral down the drain you look around, realize that when he goes out the door, he makes sure he leaves nothing behind.

The Only Story We Have

Your Aunt Clara is due to drop by in an hour. Your Gran is sending her with clothes and toys from the attic. But all the clothes will be girls' and you're feeling pretty sure the baby will be a boy. If you ask, the doctor will tell you, but you're convinced you already know.

That afternoon, lipstick on her teeth, Clara smiles and confirms that you are carrying a baby girl. This is the fifth time she has swung the needle and thread over the mountain of your belly and every time it has swung out in wide circles. "Girl," she announces, "a girl." And even though the ultrasound hasn't revealed the finer points of the baby's anatomy, even though the doctor at the clinic has never corrected you when you've said "he," you begin to wonder if there might not be something to this thread thing, although you are certain you want a boy. If only to break the unruly chain of women in this family. "We're nuts, the lot of us, Clara. Really, I want a boy. I'm sure it's a boy, the doctor would have said something, at least given me a look."

"A girl, Emma," and like "Greece," she takes up the word and carries it with her through the flat, opening curtains and stirring the lentils, the word "girl" on her lips. "Try it again," you plead but Clara simply smiles, her attention turning to the sink where she begins to wash the tea cups.

"The women in this family have always had a left breast bigger than the right." This is the kind of statement Clara is prone to make. She sets the saucers on the drying rack, looks at you. "Your Gran has to buy special bras because the left is a whole half size larger. Gets them at that Peeks Garments down off Chalk Farm."

"No need here for that," you assure her.

"It's a girl, Emma, and she might care to know."

She winks at you, dries her hands with your Bonnie Scotland tea towel, sits herself down on the floor. "Winston!" she calls and the dog comes lumbering into the kitchen. He stretches out alongside Clara and flips over, his legs up in the air. With one hand your Aunt re-pins her hair—bleached strands with a few bits of grey tucked up smartly—and with the other she pats Winston's stomach. "Dog's life," she says, a spare hairpin between her teeth, her hair pushed back into place.

"What else, Clara?"

"What needs knowing, Em?"

Clara has thirty years on you, she has whatever stigma comes with being the first baby born in an air-raided hospital, plaster and concrete falling down around her. She has a gold ankle bracelet with strings of tiny bells that jingle when she walks. What can she say to save you?

Add two cups of water, stir briskly.

At first there was a loud noise. I remember.

The bells remind me I'm here.

I have had three lovers.

This is not my natural hair colour.

Go to Greece.

Although they are a bit doughy, I enjoy the biscuits at Bread and More.

Clara pulls up her knees to her chest and looks at you like she's trying to read your mind. Winston rolls onto his side, stands up and trots out of the room. The unborn brat has begun his afternoon aerobics, ensuring your thoughts are always with him.

"What, then?" she says.

You consider what to ask her. What about the possibility of archives? Clara might have an idea of where to find some form of family history. A letter, an old pair of shoes. There must be something. Wooden boxes perhaps. You imagine yellowed oak crates spilling out of the hold of a sinking ship; crates making their way up to the beach of some desert island. Boxes full of photographs and family. People whose stories never interested you are now waiting to speak. It was your preoccupation with the picture of your father, the photo gone missing from the desk drawer, that silenced them. What can be gained or garnished from photographs anyway? But now they are there in your mind, adrift, perhaps in the damned North Sea, and looking for a place to land. Worthless, you think, except when one is marooned. And marooned you are, in Camden Town, in the city of London.

"Water," Clara had said. Big, deep pockets of water; she wasn't talking about a puddle. In your mind the archives float in and out of the offshore mist and bob scintillatingly close to land. Remember: you can barely wade and Winston has never fetched anything in water in his life. The tide is coming in, you think. With some imagination, the archival box nearly lobs up onto the beach. Its contents are that close. But still there you are with Clara in the sunlit kitchen, inhaling the smell of lentil soup with thyme, and she is telling the story of some television sitcom that struck her as funny. Now you know what must be done. Gather fishing lines and lures, long poles and a wheelbarrow for the box when you find it. Set sail for said box; there is history to be found.

Why wait for the baby to ask his first question? Make a raft and go.

Incidentals

It is your grandmother who comes through in the end, but with a fair bit of formality, as if she had been waiting for this to come about and had practiced the stoic expression and gravity of voice. "Irish" she says when hard-pressed, "my father was Irish," as if she herself could not believe it, as if taken in by all the news accounts of us and them. Consider your grandmother: her hard won self-education, her slow clipped accent, her bony hands always held just so ... clasped on her lap; cupped around the good china, baby finger poised; straight down at her sides; held together behind her back.

Consider the official portrait of the Queen hung over the end table, the collection of *The Royals* magazine. Your Gran has always wanted to take part, to belong, to feel firmly entrenched. The woman who has never travelled in her life—save to the Lowlands where she nattered on about "the Scots and their outlandish ways"—says "Irish" between clenched teeth. As if afraid the panels of the Inquisition might hear, as if she didn't buy bread from Mr. O'Connell, originally of Limerick, at eleven o'clock every third day, his immaculate shop set up across from the local library, his windows always glistening.

She runs through the details as she can recollect them. "A farmer." She pauses. "Catholic," again in a whisper, "from somewhere near Galway. He first saw my mother, called Charlotte, at the horse track when he was helping out as a stable hand. She was over from London with her father who was to buy some foals." Obviously there is more but she skips over it. Puts on the kettle, and her back to you, she adds, "I was told they both drowned."

"That's all I really know," she says. And you wonder at causality and complications, the mapping out of who we are, the importance of facts so that children can be spared the responsibility of making themselves up. And, too, you feel cheated—as if X were the unknown and now X is being scratched out on a chalkboard with something like disdain. To your grandmother the math is insignificant, an exercise in the memory of equations, old lessons she'd just as soon forget. Consider that you always liked jigs and reels, having heard them outside the door at Groggin's pub. Afraid to enter because it was said you had to respond to the doorman in Irish or he bullied you back out the door and hollered obscenities at you until you cleared the lane.

You ask your Gran for a piece of paper, make notes from what she says. You ask for a bit more. Over weak tea she confesses it was a great-aunt who raised her, and she shares what little that aunt told her some sixty years ago. Soon you've filled up three sheets of paper, slashes and arrows crisscrossing the pages.

As Small as This

There was a soft-spoken man who had a business shoeing horses and mending saddles. He opened his own shop in 1890. There was a small British girl called Charlotte who walked with a permanent limp after being thrown from a pony on her fifth birthday. Spent her sixteenth summer in Galway at the auction fairs. Her father, a devout Anglican, thought it would keep her from the public dances.

She started watching the man at the stables that summer, stood against the wall across from the open door of his shop. He would nod her way and go back to work.

In the fall she sent letters from England, to which he never responded. She wasn't even sure if she knew his name. "James O'Keefe" was written over the stable door—it was probably him. Only one other person around, a younger boy who also worked there.

Later, James and Lottie counted it out—seventeen years between them.

Her father found her letters, the "practice" ones where the handwriting was messy. He hacked off her hair with rose cutters and she ran away to Galway.

James and Lottie married.

Lived together for a year.

Had a daughter who was not christened.

And then one morning he was gone.

Flailing

Once, you watched Adam for two days straight without sleeping. Followed him from the office to his house in Clara's old Saab, its cylinders misfiring all the way. Spent the night wrapped up in your sweater, parked between street lights. Considered climbing the trellis to look in the windows.

The previous morning he'd come out with it, said "with someone," corrected himself, cleared his throat, said "married." You'd slipped out of bed, looking across the pillow at his left hand. Had you missed the ring? Nothing, not even a pale band of untanned skin. You left him lying there in your own apartment, went out wearing only dungarees, boots and a peacoat. Took Winston but forgot to put on his collar even though you had the leash. The next morning you were both on a train. Winston, out of sorts, lifted his leg against someone's luggage; they complained. The conductor, all of twenty and pimply, asked you to stand in the junction between cars. At Clara's you handed over a bag of fresh scones, mostly crushed, and asked to borrow the Saab.

Observation is as close as we get to knowing others. When set upon, people will say anything to distract you from seeing them, as if this is a survival mechanism. But watch a person long enough and you'll understand them; who we are is revealed through gesture: tilt of the head, a laid-open palm. So we don't want to be seen; we do not meet at the zoo, gloating over the gorilla cage, saying "Let me tell you exactly who I am: an insecure draftsman, an uninterested father, a philanderer, a man who loved my wife for her looks and her cooking." We do not confess. Rather, you check yourself in the glass and put forth your hand and make quips that convey charm, ease and confidence. You are selective: "My name is—; I like—; I am—; my, but and aren't the gorillas quite a size this close in life?" You joke about "Adventures in the Wild" documentaries, say "the things they show on television," "so much for the opposable thumb," and laughing, you wonder to yourself what this man might be like in bed, and if it means something when he turns his head your way.

It was as simple as looking up Adam's name in the white pages. There he was, next to a listing near Bayswater. Two days and the best you got was a good look at his entry and exit, the sound of kids in the back garden and a woman at precisely 2:15 exiting the front door in sunglasses and a camel coat with over-large lapels. Blonde and wealthy, taller than you and shapely. Not much else you could tell. Is that what you'd come to see?

What was it that drew your great-grandmother to James O'Keefe? All her patient waiting for a man over twice her age. And what did she write to him in those letters?

> *I know not who I am, I know only that the fields here fall and bend in an easy sway, I know that a horse is best ridden not pulled, nor should one lean too far forward in the saddle, a slightly angled posture is best. Today we watched the gardener take away the autumn leaves that found their way into the hedge. Bluebells are my favourite, I will write again soon.*

Was he watching her as she watched him? And what did he imagine there was to say? Did he show her the stables, placing her hand against the velvet necks of the horses, did he give them names and stories the same way Adam gave buildings history when he took you around the old houses in Bloomsbury and Fitzrovia? "I saw this foal's birth." "The houses in Bedford Square date from 1775." "This mare is raced as far as Dublin." "This church was designed by a man called Hawksmoor." Do our lovers show us these things to turn our attention from the matter at hand, or do they point out fields and columned architecture to keep from looking at themselves?

But Adam is not alone in his caginess. You remember how he'd meet you at Browning's after work and come by the flat for part of the evening, or how you'd meet at his friend's apartment to make love and have tea. You have deserted him, too, there is no denying it. There were times when he watched you gathering your things, your body language saying that it's too much, that for the sake of sanity, you have to go.

Lottie left too. And came back. So that one morning come May, James looked up and found her again in her usual place, her back against the wall of Leary's abattoir. Changed as girls change over the course of a year. And you wonder: was he waiting for her to mature, or was he waiting for her to make her own way to the open door of his shop and, once there, ask to stay? Maybe the odd bleating or bay from Leary's, or a cow's panicked groan, would distract him. The horses in the stable stirring, their nostrils growing wide with the smell of fresh blood. James would soothe them, run his hand along their necks, make clucking sounds in their ears. A second laboured bellow might cause him to look up sharply, as if Leary wasn't doing his job, as if the cow's death was taking too long. James would look angrily to the abattoir then, and there Lottie would be, unflinching.

So it is historical. We have stood in towns and cities around animals domestic and wild. We've leaned against concrete walls and thought of love while behind us animals crashed to their knees, eyes rolling back in their heads until they were blind and dead. With our fingers knuckling the ape's cage, we've clicked our tongues and said "hoohoo" as if it were the most natural of sounds. We've watched each other studiously and made lists of intent, as if our course of action were rational. As if we ourselves were in charge of it all.

Rereading the Great Romances

It went thus: They met at London Zoo, unassuming. Others were about. He offered to escort her along to see the marmots, "Here, just down the way." Overhead in wide wire cages exotic birds preened and wielded great feathers, the more colourful ones upending from turns in flight.

The next week, he and she walked hand-in-hand along the canal towpath. The wind was up and his coat flapped around his legs. Polystyrene containers lay clustered in murky puddles near the bushes. The air was heavy with the lingering smell of sausage and chips. The woman—we'll call her Emma—thought the man somewhat appealing but she had given up hope that she would ever find true-ish love. Truth be told, she was holding out for one of the Royals—Andrew, perhaps. Maybe he could overlook her overworked hands, her discount Marks and Spencer briefs. Things had yet to go her way but looking to love was as reasonable as entering the Lotto. Declining to do that, she chanced her odds elsewhere. Later she would look back and recollect that her hair was longer then, full. One might say, "streaming." Her penchant was for flowing skirts with simple blouses, a sprig of a daisy in her hair. This man, she noted, had a certain sheen; he was well manicured.

They entered a pub's dark oak doorway; the place was full. The barman at The Old Stand poured them pints, saying they had no more Samuel Smith, or perhaps that the taps needed changing—either way, the man did not have his usual. She had whiskey as well as lager, which was unlike her, then she followed with a second pint. Something in the mix, she thought later. They were forced to stand near a cubby at the farthest end from the door. His hair fell over his eye a few times and by nine P.M. she was brushing it back for him, flirting wildly while fingering the cigarette burns on the balustrade adjacent. She briefly considered Prince Andrew and the possibility of Buckingham Palace, stand seats at polo matches, but this man had her transfixed. By ten she felt it was all a bit fuzzy. And they gave themselves up utterly to love.

What Is Yours and What Is Taken

Your Gran states that she has no pictures, no interest in her history at all. You explain about the imagined archives, inquire about a wedding photo, a date at least. She doesn't know where her parents married, or when. If it was formal at all. "He was Catholic," she says, as if this is an explanation for the lack of clarity, a map of improbability. "Never the twain" is what you think she'll say, but she purses her lips and sorts through papers as requested. You stand over her thinking that this is all wrong, thinking that the baby might not even care, that the world is changing and borders are being redrawn daily. You've read that on average a woman has nine great-grandchildren, that of the nine only two will even know her name. Why work at beating the odds, why care when he will have maths and spelling, all the rules of football and eventually the Sunday crossword to concern himself with? Instead, hand out photos of total strangers around the flat, reinvent everyone.

Pulling out a box, your grandmother opens it tentatively, as if it might trigger some sensitive mechanism and explode. There are school reports from her junior courses at Claremont, East End London. There is a postcard from her mother's first trip out to Galway. A group of overdressed women stand with parasols on the beach. "After they married and James disappeared, Lottie returned to England but she would go back to Galway and wait for him every year around April." In the box there are shells and letters from Granddad, there are bits of embroidery from lessons and little else. In contrast, the attic is full. Your grandfather couldn't doodle on a napkin those last years without Gran folding it up in a plastic bag for preservation.

You leave Gran in charge of detailing her life with your grandfather. Ask her to make up a short history for the baby. Pictures and stories about Gramps.

You remember that your mother said he had a way of tapping his thigh when he sat quietly, how he sat quietly most of his days. This makes you want people around you, you'd like to resurrect the dead, ask ridiculous questions, set everyone on edge. In the photos set up around the house, nailed into the rust-coloured living room walls, your grandfather is always surrounded. The wide grinning faces of men arm-in-arm on a ship's flight deck, swaggering together against the slate-grey wall of the boat. "He sang songs," your grandmother tells you and you ask her to write them down, sorry you never heard them, curious to know which ones.

Do men and children so take over our lives that we forget where we came from? You want to ask her this. Instead, you wait while she smooths her skirt, stands then sits, unsure of what she should show you next. Outside a group of children are laughing and making whooping calls, screaming as they run. Will these small moments be forgotten? Do children pack away their spirits at the end of the day, wash up from having thrashed through the dirty garage and fall asleep, letting it all go? Do we lose our most vital moments so that we can remember noon feedings, the correct positioning of mouth to breast?

You have easily ten thousand minuscule and mundane moments with Adam tucked safely away. You meander through them often enough. You have ten of grandmother: at Christmas; at the foot of the ladder; in the window to the back garden; at your first and only, miserable swimming lesson, her arms crossed as if the look of the water made her cold. Those and a few others. So remember her now, staring wistfully at your granddad's photo. Her collection of silver spoons hung just to the left.

The Disappeared

There are a few facts to go by now, the rest is left to your imagination. You know that after James left her, Charlotte returned to London but made trips back to Galway every year waiting for him to come find her. But where would she go? Maybe she stood across the street from the stable shop and willed him to come back to her. The shop changed names, changed hands, perhaps it was torn down and turned into a residence. Still she would go and wait, lean against the concrete wall outside the abattoir and listen to the cries of animals, counting totals for the day and then the week. Six pigs, four cows. It was a slow business. One day, tired of looking at the grey house opposite her, she might have walked around the corner to watch the men go about their work. Anything to take her mind off the breezeless day, the stone wall that faced her.

Because she was English, most of the locals would not have made time for her and she probably didn't make any for them. *He knows I'm here*, she might have reasoned, *this is the anniversary of the day we married. When he is ready, he will come.* And maybe there was a time, a year, when she thought she saw him: a broad stretch of back framed by thin brown suspenders making his way up to the bridge. She would have stood her ground, thinking *he knows where I'm waiting and I will not give him the satisfaction of going after him.* You imagine she pushed her back farther into the cement wall as if for strength, pushed hard enough that she could feel her bones bearing down against it.

You think: Lottie knew who she was and she knew James.

She believed he would come back to her, that he would have a reason for his absence. But even if there was no reason, even if he refused to explain himself with so much as a word, you somehow think she would have taken him back. Maybe she missed the blue and green lines of his veins, the ones that ran from wrist to elbow and up again. He'd first kissed her on her wrist. Not on the back of her hand, as would be proper, but on the pulse of her wrist, turning her hand over and leaning in, feeling how readily she trembled.

Consider the Species

Consider the species: men. Consider our need of them. The modern world provides us with evidence of all-female lizard colonies reproducing themselves, of a small brown speckled bird whose males no longer require a penis. Evolution has taken a turn; it's gone off in entirely new directions. Who would have thought it possible? That we could do our best without men, that we could try to make way? If evolution has brought you here, led you up to the oak doorway outside Browning's Book Sellers, if it has unfurled itself like a flag, at least you can see it, the wind whipping up all around you as if to remind you that the elements hold sway. So you progress in spite of the weather. You unlock the door and begin to work. You put everything in order—receipt books and pens, the mail that was dropped through the slot in the morning. You turn on the lights outside the store, turn on the heater and plug in the kettle. You go back outside in the wind and hang a brass plate that says "Open" onto its shiny hook. You make sales in the morning, take stock in the afternoon.

Adam is now calling once or twice a day. Yesterday, he stood inside the door of your flat and said it's still too soon for him to know. "Know what?" you snapped, Adam acting as if he was debating whether to walk or take a taxi, Adam standing in front you looking like he hadn't slept for a week.

"The other day, watching you in the bath, I didn't want to leave you. Em, it's breaking my heart." But he did leave, and you point that out to him, you stand in the door with your soon-to-be-born child between you. "But you did, Adam. You did leave." And he shrugs, looks down at the space between his feet. This is his half-hearted commitment, his close-fisted "I'm doing the best that I can."

Now, on your last day at Browning's, between browsing customers and the occasional sale, you wonder: is this progress after all? What is progress and how does one measure such a precocious thing? You started *here* alone and ended up *here* still alone. How much progress have you made? And then all the infighting, how Adam wants you to forgive him, how he hates that he can't quite be the man he wants to be. There are discussions, there are accusations, there is the pacing, which leads from back to forth and round again, a trench of tread marks almost visible on the living room carpet. You are making a baby, together you are making a baby and progress might have its way with that child, but what way will that be? His eyesight better than Adam's? Absence of a cowlick over the temples? His reserve stronger than yours? Or maybe, unlike his parents, he will not need for anything or anyone at all.

Marianne Nickerson was your best friend in school. She had two parents and never gloated about it. One summer you sat in the treehouse her father had built her and you demanded a list of what was good about a father. You made a sort of mantra of her happiness and goaded your mother into trying to follow suit. Treehouse/Piggyback/Captain sailor games/Chases bogeymen/Has an office/Presents/Smells nice/Likes my fish.

You ended up with an old tire hanging from the oak tree in the back garden; a tire your mother bought at MacKay's Garage, rolling it home some eight blocks to please you. The rope swung up into the branches, and even now, you can still see your mother standing on the low branch in her beige trousers and white shirt, trying to fasten the loop. Still, every other time you hopped on it, the rope unravelled and the tire fell the two feet to the ground. Your mother would come out and dust you off, then she'd climb back up into the tree again, pulling the rope behind her.

This is what leads you to believe that there is always some consolation for what comes undone. Your mother came out into the garden when you called her, she dutifully went back up into the tree. And where are you now that the rope has at last fallen, and the tire been given away? First it was the struggle for adulthood, all that incessant wanting, and now it's the weary reversal. How quickly you'd trade your practical loafers and the stacked washer-dryer for that thin rubber tire swinging out in wide circles over the back garden. How quickly you'd trade womb for womb, giving your small body back to your mother rather than bear this child alone.

Paternity

It was not altogether impossible to do, you'd just never considered doing it. But we live, after all, in the modern age—there are detectives now, and you can ring Information in every city if you choose to make a day of it. And the phone is already in your hand. "A listing please, for Henry William Westcott. No, I've no address. None? Thanks, then."

You put down the phone and stare at it hanging in its cradle. You think, why not make a go of it, see if I can find him. You are bringing a child into the world without the benefit of a father. Now would be the time to decide if you actually missed out on anything at all.

You get an old map of the country from the dresser drawer, smooth it out on the kitchen table. It occurs to you that this might be what they do in war: take a Biro, start circling towns and cities, all the places one intends to conquer. You start with the summer house where your mother first met him. She was working for a family down the next lane. The father was a banker and there were three young girls. Your mother was hired on to work in the kitchen but spent most of the summer escorting the children into town for treats. She met Henry on the walk along the pier. He already knew her name.

You ring up the exchange for Southampton, circle it on the map. You have a rough idea of an address for the Westcott cottage, and after an elongated conversation with an operator called Barry, you end up with the number of a local fish-and-chip shop. In the summer the chip shop owners open a tourist stand inside the restaurant. It's off-season yet but Barry says you can ring them and give them a try.

Helen is frying whitefish but she'll be right with you. Kevin is happy enough to keep you entertained on the phone. You hear his breathing and the odd shout over his shoulder and then a question in a Liverpool accent about how long it's been since you've been out that way. Over the spit and gurgle of the fryer Helen says she knows the Westcott house and has an idea about who lives there, she'll look it up in the local directory. Then she sets the phone down so that you can listen to the fryer gurgle and flay.

A woman with a musical voice picks up the cottage phone and informs you "No, the Westcotts have sold, after the Missus died, but the son still comes back and rents down the way." You make something up, feign familiarity and residence in Canada. "Just visiting, been years." She is drinking from a glass as you explain, you hear the rattle of ice, her hurried swallow. "A cousin, you say. Oh how nice. No, I can't be sure, dear, but try the law registry, I have the name of his firm on a card. One minute. I think he's in Norwich now."

Rereading the Great Romances 2

It's Jane Eyre all over again, insomuch as her hair is tightly coiffed and she works long hours keeping house and tending to other people's children. And too, she is somewhere between plain and almost beautiful, although it takes a certain light and long hours for others to see it. But we are in Southampton and not anywhere near the moors, although at times the air is thick here.

The boy—we'll call him Henry—lives in a London house with two kitchens. In the summers his family heads for the coast to spend a month gazing across the Channel at the Isle of Wight. She is a nanny for the Dawson family who spend their summers in a two-hundred-year-old cottage at the end of a long narrow lane. The families are acquainted. When the boy meets the girl out by the pier he bows to her as if she is some of kind of royalty, although he stops short of kissing her hand. "Elizabeth" she says, although to tease her he immediately calls her Betty and she laughs even though she hates the name. "There's a bonfire on the weekend," he says, could she get away from the Dawsons and come?

This is how she finds herself, in her one good dress, standing in the wind with a boy from London. He takes her hand and runs with her towards the water, then they back up and run towards the tide again. Behind them the beachfire crackles and hisses, as the other boys add more wood.

This is a port town, and in the high season the sun spreads itself evenly over everything as if the tourist board had commanded it: over the boats bobbing amiably offshore, over the old city gate at the end of Highstreet, over the shops with their bright red and yellow awnings. "Look," he says, showing her around the town, "there's fat Mrs. Hendry and her four bulldogs, there's Ken the fisherman who'll buy us a few jars if we give him an extra five pounds." "Look," he says, gesturing to the sun shining on the grotty old city walls, pointing so that she looks away, kissing her when she turns back around. "Come on," he says, "there's something else I want to show you." He takes her home. The summer house is huge and the floorboards in the entryway are creaky. But there are no half-mad wives up in the attic, there are no carriage rides through the fens. There is only Henry, whom she wants to see again, and a sinking feeling she mistakes for love.

In the Beginning

Six days to the due date and you are on a train. It's four hours from London to Norwich and you are nearly there. Outside, the East Anglian countryside rolls out like plush carpet in every direction, Norwich proper popping up in the middle of it like a medieval fortress tucked inside crumbling flint walls. Later, standing on the edge of a roundabout on the outskirts of town, you think to yourself: this child will have a history and it will be placed in his hand. First your own father, then the lot from Ireland.

On Haymarket you enter a grey stone building. You take the elevator up two floors, avoiding its full-length mirrors. You step into a reception room and look around. A man in a suit is standing in front of the receptionist's desk; he's sorting through a stack of papers.

"Very good, Sir," the receptionist says.

He says, "And this one as well," handing over a sheaf of papers. "Oh, and if Cindy calls, let her know I'm on my way."

"Of course, Mr. Westcott, I will."

You turn around, follow him into the elevator, which is on its way down. It's already full, but you squeeze in, everyone's eyebrows going up at the advanced state of your pregnancy, a grumble from somewhere in the back as people move to accommodate you. Mr. Westcott smells like cigarette smoke, his tie is askew and his hair receding. In one hand he carries a briefcase, and he's looking down at it as if considering the contents. You've the same colour hair and have inherited his long hands.

And that is about it. He looks over at you suddenly, as if aware of some oddity; you smile and he looks away. The doors open and you both exit the building. The air is fresh here, the street is cobbled. He crosses towards the side street and, already out of breath, you pause for a second, then start off again in the hope of catching up to him.

You decide again that this child will have everything. *Here is Winston, our dog, your grandma, your great-grandma, my aunt Clara, her goldfish, the budgie Sam. This is Aaron, the grocer who brings in your Pablum, next door is a cellist practising Bach, the best scones come from Chalk Farm Bakery and you will have them in plenty.* He will have everything, but after sleepless nights spent tossing in the tent of your flannel nightie, you have come to realize he will also have nothing. Walks in Bayswater past Georgian homes: *Here is where your father lives with his family, notice the* Independent *on the doorstep, the well-hedged shrubbery. Victoria likes muted drapery so as not to shock the neighbours. They're out of bananas at Sainsbury's so you must eat squash purée. The scones have gone up in price, we can't afford them. You have no grandfather, and no, your father is not dead.*

On the street in Norwich, passing under the shadow of a gothic spire, you follow your father as he clip-clops along, humming some song you can almost recognize. You look at the shape of his back, the slope of his shoulders, you watch his long and hurried gait. *Ah-hem,* you want to shout, *Excuse me, sir,* but he is just two steps beyond you and now that the moment is here you are not sure what to say to him. You want to tell him who you are and that others will be following you. A son. His grandson. Flesh and blood. You want to draw a concrete line from one person to another and then on to another, you want it mapped out and agreed upon by all parties. You want, at least, for him to offer you his hand. Then you'll pack your bags and make a last-ditch effort to fill in the family tree. Go to Dublin and then to Galway, even if you have to give birth on the bloody boat.

Handing Over

You imagined the day you'd tell Adam about the baby a thousand times before you actually got as far as Bayswater to do it. Now you are following the man you believe is your father, getting ready for a declaration of a different kind. You watch his arm swinging the briefcase alongside him, you measure the span of his back. You imagine your slight frame must have come from your mother, but your hands are like his. Mr. Westcott turns the corner at Bedford Street and you follow, all the unknowns, all your lost history clanging away behind you like pots and pans on a stretch of rope. It's a wonder he doesn't hear the ruckus, this man walking in front of you like a question.

You follow Henry William Westcott to a restaurant and he looks over his shoulder a good five or six times. Finally he pauses, four feet from the door, the maitre d' taking a step forward, expectant. Mr. Westcott stops and turns to face you, steps out from the entryway and towards the street. A slim blonde woman appears suddenly in the doorway, half in the sunlight, half shadowed by the green awning. She has a menu in her hand, big silvery bangles all up one arm. Cindy, you suppose. So thrilled to see him she got up from the table. You walk towards Mr. Westcott and she watches. You open your mouth but he puts his hand up into the space between you. "I'm not your man." There is a considerable silence.

Dumbfounded, you find yourself nodding, as if agreement is all that's possible. Around you, flowers bloom brightly in stone planters. The hum of lunchtime conversations and a light piano tune from the restaurant washes over your head. You notice his grip on the briefcase, the white knuckles, the almond shape of his eyes. Over in the doorway Cindy stands, arms crossed, her mouth a straight pink line. Perhaps she imagines you are a client. "I'm pregnant," you say to him, stating the obvious, almost as if this is Adam all over again. "I said, I'm not your man," and with that Henry William Westcott turns on his heel and walks inside. "Suppose not," is all you manage to muster.

You sit on a bench outside the eatery, Chez Michele, disbelieving. How many Wescotts, you wonder, can there be? Or did he recognize you, decide: here is my daughter, better fend her off? The eyes maybe. Maybe the eyes were the same. Or was he so indiscriminate that he thought you were a past lover, the woman he'd met at the bar just over eight months ago and had taken up to one of the rooms, paying by credit card or on account? Either way he is disappointing, and just this once you had wanted to avoid disappointment. Even if he'd said, "I see" or "I had no idea." Or "There is no room in my life for a child, a grandchild, children. I am a busy barrister and have too much at stake," even that would have sufficed. You might have had lunch together, perhaps you would have felt satisfied with his conversation, maybe his observations would have been kind.

You write a note and you say: *Mr. Henry Westcott. I am your daughter by Elizabeth whom you knew at Southampton. I wanted to say hello.* You send the note in with the maitre d'. You wait. He doesn't come out. When you finally check your watch, gauging how much time you'll need to make the London train, you realize you've been sitting here for three hours. There is undoubtedly a back door and although you are tempted, you don't feel the desire to confirm it. You imagine he'd have left through the kitchen, irritating the chefs, maybe losing his balance as he came around the stainless steel counter. "Whoa there, mate," someone might have said. Cindy in her black heels and blue dress stepping carefully over the tile behind him.

On the bench outside Chez Michele, you feel huge and grotesque, your knees angling out and your skirt pulled tight as a sheet across them. You push your hands hard into your thighs and heave yourself up. Then you start off across town, heading for Thorpe Road and the six P.M. London train.

An Architectural Tour of Georgian Homes

Adam liked to take you on tours of old English homes, the Georgian style being his favourite. As the train takes you back to London, whizzing past stately hilltop houses, you remember this, how you were happy simply being with him, how excited he'd get when he showed you something new. You liked the names the best: Chiswick House, Holkham Hall, Chilington, Ormesby, Dunham Massey, the engraved plaques in front of the houses all polished and gleaming as if grandeur is tied to the act of naming. So you renamed them all yourself: "the house we will never live in," and too, "the house we will never live in" and again—Adam opening up the door to an old home his firm was renovating—"the house we will enter, walk around in like ghosts, but will most certainly never live in."

"They call it Bedford House," Adam had said, and you remember how he walked you down the hall and into the dining room, how he ran his hand over the worn wine-coloured wallpaper and how you listened halfheartedly to the list of things yet to be done: "replace some of the coade stone on the exterior, reslate the roof, reinforce the supporting wall, refinish the wood in all the rooms." And then he walked you into the empty master bedroom, a room made spare and cold by the lack of furnishings, and he showed you how the wood floor sloped in parts and how it would have to be replaced, and he pointed out the coved ceilings, the old fireplace with its heavy iron grate, and he mentioned the fruit trees in the yard. And all the while you were wondering who'd lived here and when they had left, and how they looked out on the world from behind their sash windows, and did they have children and how many, and why, when they had a home, did they ever leave?

Lottie might have lived in a home like that. A grand Georgian home with a garden and, somewhere out back, stables. She grew up with her father's horses, she grew up with servants and a cook, she probably had a fair-sized bedroom: windows to the back lawn, bright patterned wallpaper covering the walls. And maybe she went back home after her trips to Galway feeling as defeated and embarrassed as you feel now. Maybe it's the same thing—the idea that you're not wanted, that you've offered yourself up for naught. Lottie would have gone back to her father after the baby was born and James left her. Her father was probably the one who sent the baby away. It must have felt like a prison, that home; or maybe it was the only real home she ever knew? You wonder if Lottie's father tried to keep her from going back to Galway, if he locked her in her room, if he pulled her by the arm until she was bruised and screaming. Maybe this is what fathers do. Muddle about believing they want what's best for you. And how often did she visit her little girl? Did the aunt send letters from East London? *She is walking. Her hair is brown and full. Her first word was honey, she likes to put her fingers in the jar.*

Or maybe there were no letters at all. Lottie thinking she had nothing to give her child except the annual totter and pitch of the boat ride from Liverpool to Dublin and the carriage ride on to the coast. Every year Lottie must have gone back into her father's house a little more defeated. But at least she had this: for a year she'd lived with James in two rooms he couldn't afford, a quarter mile from his shop. For a year she had everything she wanted.

In Evidence

"What will it prove?" she asks.

Your mother is at her crafts again, leaning over her almost complete gothic birdhouse, squinting under the lamplight. The tea tray sits steaming on the settee against the far wall but she hasn't budged save to push her glasses up her nose and affix the final cloister piece in place. You turn on a nearby lamp to illuminate more of the room.

"It will be something to give him," you suggest.

"Who?"

"The baby." You move to the sofa where you plump up two pillows for your back.

"Can't it wait, Emma?" and her sigh has more to do with her task than with yours.

"No. It can't, Mum." You exhale, eye the tea but feel too tired to get up. You sum it up for her, enunciating each word: "The closer I get to the due date the more I wholeheartedly panic."

"Well, as your mother," and at this she stands up straight and looks right at you with some authority, "I forbid you to go. It's irresponsible. For the baby's sake." She pulls the chain on her desk lamp and, squinting again, looks around for the tea.

"You can't forbid me."

"I just did."

There was a time when you would have listened to her with the unconditional assumption of her authority. Wear the extra sweater to fend off the cold, wear braids to school in summer because they're darling, ride your bike without training wheels because it's time. Always a criticism. "You can't, you should, it's not good enough." With Adam your mistakes were too like her own for comment. Until she couldn't restrain her anger any longer.

"You think you're in love?" she had asked, incredulous, the night she, Clara and Adam were first supposed to meet. You had planned a dinner out and Adam had yet to arrive. You remember the waiter at San Remo's backing away from the table with his water jug, your mother trying to contain herself, her face red and pinched.

"I am." And you smoothed out the white linen tablecloth, rearranged your utensils.

"Love?" she reiterated. "Love?"

"Elizabeth—" Clara had interrupted, but your mother went on, ignoring her.

"Can you define it, Emma? Can you describe love?" Her mouth with its orangey lip colour trembling.

"I can, Mother."

"Well perhaps you could just point?" The empty space beside you, her way of reminding you of the inevitable. Her way of bearing her scars.

"I'm going to Dublin," you repeat now. "Clara is minding Winston, Browning's already given me leave."

Your mother sets her cup and saucer on the settee, straightens a perfectly straight photograph of herself and Clara from when they were in their teens.

"No."

"I didn't have to tell you, Mum."

"Yes, you did."

You want to tell her about Henry. That he's a lawyer, that he could stand to lose some weight around the middle. That you're sorry if going after him was a betrayal, that now you know paternity doesn't equal virtue. You want to tell your mother you sat on a bench outside an upscale eatery for hours, the pigeons huddling around you, finally figuring out, after all these years, that she did her best, that his absence wasn't for lack of wanting. Finally understanding that she did not make him disappear.

You push yourself forward on the couch and start to stand up. You move towards the desk, turn on the lamp to look again at her birdhouse cathedral. All your will intent on your decision, regardless of whether or not she understands.

"It's amazing," you say, admiring the intricacy of the work, thinking that she and Adam have architecture in common, imagining the strained arts-and-crafts conversations that might have occurred at family meals.

"It's nothing."

And with that she comes back to the desk in the middle of the room, checking the last few pieces she'd glued in.

"Mum, listen," you repeat, thinking about the trip again, hoping the two of you can come to an understanding, "it's just that I have nothing to give this baby."

After a minute, when she hasn't answered you or turned away from her work, you decide to leave.

"Be back Wednesday," you say. And you're out the door.

The Pub Once Again

"They won't let you fly," Adam chortles.

"I'm off to the ferry at three."

"You're serious?" He tips back the pint glass and swallows, eyes not straying from your face.

"Yup."

"Bloody incredible."

Outside the snug, two young men in suits are arguing about European Union politics over lunch. They start to get louder; one bangs his drink on the table.

"Yer full of it."

"Fuck yourself."

Andy the barman is filling peanut bowls from a bag. He's minding his own business but mutters "eejits" under his breath loud enough to be heard. The door of your snug is open so Andy smiles in at you, his thin black hair combed sideways over a balding patch. He reminds you of a working-class Mr. Browning. The two men are still at it.

"If Blair didn't have his head up his arse—"

"No, Pete, more like if you read the feckin' papers—"

"How's yer pints, boys?" Andy asks the two men.

"Off to Dublin," Adam says while patting your belly, which is a visible mound behind the tabletop. "I could tell you stories," he says in the direction of your prodigious womb. "Give you a genealogy. My grandfather was a stone mason," he pauses, "there's some story about a half-mad aunt who became a nun—" and then looking up at you, "I swear Em, you don't have to go to Dublin." Just then, Andy walks in to see after your pints. "Off to Dublin," Adam says, pointing his thumb in your direction.

"Happy trails to the Missus," Andy says, as if you're Adam's wife. The staff had figured you were lovers after you started drinking there two years ago, what with the snug, the hushed conversations, the fantastic amount of touching in those months before the pregnancy. "The Missus" was probably an in-joke, their way of making you feel at home.

"Missus," Adam whispers after Andy has gone, grinning at you. "Victoria'd love to hear that."

"Adam, I wouldn't be your Missus if you were the last and only man—"

"All right, enough." He leans over and kisses your temple. "Is your mother going with you?"

And after all possible chaperones have been ruled out one by one—"Winston, even?"—he offers to take the afternoon off as long as he can catch the last flight home that night. Just to get you there safe.

"Like you got me here?" You dig in your bag for a fiver. "Really?"

"Em . . . Tonight I'm telling Victoria about the baby."

"All right, well tomorrow I'll be at the Dublin archives picturing you locked out of the house, wearing the flowerpot that she threw at your head."

You lean over to kiss him, then pull your cardigan up over your shoulders. "I'll be fine," you say. "See me out the door, will you?"

He finishes off his pint in a long swallow and you head to the door.

"Good day, Andy."

"Good day, now, Missus. All the best on your trip."

Outside, Adam pulls your cardigan around you, stretching the fabric, fastening each button until at the top he realizes he's missed one along the way. He goes at it again, close enough you can smell the aftershave you gave him a year ago Christmas, see the stubble coming up around his chin. Suddenly you are kissing him and all the old feelings are flitting about in you—there is even the familiar taint of beer on his tongue. Here we are again, you think. Giving into it as if this is some consolation. "Emma," Adam says, because there is nothing else to say here, "Em." So you pull away because you are not on the same team after all, you aren't even playing the same game. He has told you a hundred times that he is unhappy with Victoria, that the kids are what keeps him home, that she is a good mother but that over the years she's become cold and distant from him. Maybe he loves this in you, your acquiescence, the easy adoration, the way you light up against your will when he comes to the flat.

"I have to go," you say, pulling back from him. And because he is the same Adam who once left you waiting for two hours in Kensington Park, he drops his arms to his sides and steps away. Turning the corner, taking the steps down to the tube station, overwhelmed by what you've set out to do, you find yourself thinking: *This once, please come after me, Adam. Pick your sorry self up and come.*

Passive Resistance

You assume James did nothing because, to you, he is a blank page. Your grandmother has told you a few things, but they are merely the facts of history as it happened around him: war and what-it-is we read in books. When pressed to speak of her father, your grandmother pursed her lips and shook her head. James O'Keefe of Galway, son of James and Angus before him. Because no one can prove otherwise, you assume he did nothing while all around him civil and world wars were raging. Zeppelins were sailing over London skies. James was probably avoiding it all, sitting it out on the coast of the Atlantic, his legs hung over rocks, his feet just touching the sea. Mata Hari indignant right up to her execution, tank battles booming over in Cambrai— you imagine he heard nothing of any of it. Maybe he wished the fighting away, maybe he only wanted silence. You can't say, you find it hard to imagine. You have created a man out of rumour and hearsay: His world was small: himself, his father and the town's horses. You imagine there was a foal he was saving to buy once he could find an acre to build a decent stable.

It wasn't that he didn't see Charlotte watching him those first two years before they married; rather, he didn't have anything to say to her. Maybe he conjured up conversations, listened in on couples as they walked along Salthill Road. Nothing seemed appropriate, none of the premeditated introductions rang true. He must have believed that all he had to offer was his hands and the work he did with them. Saying nothing to her those years, the slight English girl who came to the races, who sometimes came to the stable to watch him. After she started writing he probably kept the letters. Busy with work, oiling saddles, he wrote back to her in his head. *Fair last week. Saving up for a mare. Would like my own stables. Mr. Fay has given up his setter and the dog has come to the shop to stay. I give him the bones from O'Leary's, a gentle peace between us.*

Above all else, James valued loyalty—this is the way you see it—but not the intransigent loyalty of cause. The country around him raged and vaulted, perhaps a gun was set to his head and, if what your grandmother said was true, he was told by those whose political opinions differed from his to pack up his possessions and leave. But where was there to go? He might have refused to acknowledge the civil war in Ireland or he might have taken part in it. But his loyalty was most likely to that place, a set of solid wood stalls he'd made himself, posts and meat hooks for hanging saddles borrowed from across the way. This was what he had. And there was a girl—a woman—who waited, would return every year during the horse fairs and races. Maybe he hoped he would find the words to tell her what he was feeling, nightly undressing her in his mind, going to sleep on a straw pile and blanket, her pale freckled arms opening up to him in dreams.

Mucking About

People mill around the ferry looking excited, a mix of overnight-bag locals and foreign travellers with huge rucksacks and unwashed hair. A demure blonde in the corner by the lifeboat information board is being entertained by two rowdy Irish boys in their late teens. She is giggling and throws back her hair. The boat is ready to burst from all the pent-up longing—to get over the water safely and on to something else, to get home, to get the girl, to get dinner. People tap their toes in the long cafeteria line, hands holding onto steel guide rails, as if the act of leaving the English shore were equivalent to parting the Red Sea. Only the most subtle chortle of engine and wave wash can be heard beneath the din of conversation. Everyone has a go at making themselves familiar with their surroundings: lounge A, lounge B, this way to the arcade, bar here, loo through there, baby changing room here and come one and all to the smell of burgers and chicken. All corridors lead this way: Chicken Breast with Potato is on special. On the wall are a series of small framed signs, one reading:

> *Snacks are good.*
> *Food for the soul.*

You sit and watch the cafeteria crowd, a slow progression of people as unhappy as if they were in food queues during the war. If only they weren't so hungry, if only they'd planned a snack. It's one pound fifty for an apple. A captive audience does that to the price of fruit. Highway robbery, you think, but still you're peckish. You excuse yourself, get up, wedge past the couple at the end of your row of plush highback chairs. People turn in their seats to let you pass. This is how it is with pregnant women: immediate thoroughfares. Even Browning at the bookstore has been treating you as if you were as fragile as an egg. "Excuse me," you say and the knees practically go up to their chins to let you by. "Sorry there." All for a lousy apple.

But then you change your mind, come out from between knees and velour seats with a new resolve. You're not even sure how it happens. A pound fifty an apple, you think, almost two quid, resolving not to buy the apple you crave and resolving never to be taken again by what you don't need and/or can't afford: expensive fruit, a nice house in a respectable part of the city, a man who comes complete with a wife and children. This, you realize at last, is about the power of persuasion and it comes in many forms: Adam saying he will leave Victoria; your mum saying he won't; and even this, the bright pyramid of apples in the cafeteria cooler.

You turn back towards the chair you just left, wedging yourself down eight feet of a sloping aisle, pushing your belly along, the ferry just underway. You've finally convinced yourself you will not give in. The resolve to get here has taken years.

Freight

For the first two hours of the trip you sit in the ferry's main seating area feeling sickly. The chair is padded and barely accommodates your hips. Once you are wedged in you decide there's no leaving unless the whole ship starts to sink and lifeboats are called for. Still, after a spate of people-watching and fidgeting you give up and head for the shop to browse the magazines and buy a Lilt. "Excuse me," you say, bumping into the shelf of souvenir paperweights opposite the magazines. "Sorry there," says a young Irish girl eyeing your belly as she wedges her way past, heading towards the music magazines. The girl stands beside you and starts flipping through *NME*. "Sorry," says someone else as she bumps into you and so you move into the hallway where people can get by and you look out the porthole at the choppy grey waves, hoping for good weather to land.

It is May the twenty-fourth today—that's the date on your ferry ticket. The original due date was yesterday until the doctor put it back almost a week. Everyone here and at the terminal is looking at you like Adam did, like your mother did, as if you are a time bomb about to explode. Even the man sitting next to you in the lounge was afraid to brush past you, making a big production of exiting at the opposite end of the aisle. Where was Lottie, you wonder, when she was at this stage with your Gran? Was she living in a house with James, preparing herself for what was about to happen?

You have never been to Ireland, although you'd meant to go once with Adam. It was to be a getaway weekend; Victoria had gone off to her mother's with the kids. You figured on a hotel in the city and a walking tour of Dublin the next morning. Instead you got stuck in Wales on the way to the ferry, the car breaking down in Llangollen, where you spent most of the day at the town's one repair shop, Adam trying to assist the man with the intricacies of Victoria's BMW. You remember you'd come back to the garage with a light green dress from a tiny boutique. Pulling it out of the bag you held it in front of you, turning around, thinking to impress him with the style. There was grease on his lapel, which you found rather funny. Laughing, you asked Adam to look at the dress. He saw the price tag and became livid. "And who," he said, "did you expect to pay for that?" Everything went wrong from that point on and you spent the night at some ramshackle B&B, arguing. The weekend came to a quick close.

The North Sea you know: tales of oil rigs going up in furious explosions, seen from the coast where emergency crews always stood ready. Your first real boyfriend, Bobby, was a shift worker who sealed the drums. Scrubbed himself clean even when he wasn't working. Had raw pink bits on worn-through parts of his skin. The North Sea was a cold and grey expanse that was broadcast on television, filmed from helicopters that swayed back and forth over whatever industrial accident or coastal crisis was being reported. But this is different, you prefer this, the Irish Sea and its gentle lapping in long, slow swooshes. Almost a metronome back and forth as you pace the hallways, almost a cradle rocked in full swing. Out the porthole a dark blue sky is tucked up against the curling waves, waves like hands saying hello or like the small white-crested curl of a fist. This is the kind of water that invites you to dive into it, water that pulls you down.

What's Left Us

Dublin

Grafton Street is crowded, the street lamps throwing out light in wide, round circles. Cheerful-seeming people come and go from restaurants and clubs. Every now and again a pedestrian smiles politely as you make your way along, your map resting on the tableau of your belly, your head bobbing up to check street signs and take in faces. You turn left down South Anne Street and spot a well-lit phone box to call, confirm your arrival with Clara.

"All's well, I'm a few blocks from the main street."

"Your mother's in a panic."

"Not to worry, I'm tired but well. I'll ring again tomorrow."

But you are feeling a bit under the weather and are tired enough from the long ferry ride that you think a tea should do it and so head back onto Grafton Street, retracing your steps to Bewleys. Once ensconced in the bench seat, with the table pushed out to offer you enough room, you rethink your situation. And do so with a certain glee. You have arrived and accents abound, around you a flurry of people come in and go out of the room, steaming cups and saucers clattering precariously on their trays. The baby is due in four days, the baby room is ready, your body is beyond ready but you are not. So be it. At least this once you've thought of no one save yourself and the baby. Your mother had forbidden you to travel but you'd left regardless. Adam had tried to bait you with the apocalyptic confrontation at hand: "I'll tell Victoria about the baby." And maybe he will, perhaps he won't, either way he's not a part of what's happening here.

"All right Miss?" A young girl clears your tea cup from the table, runs a cloth over the wood.

"Fine, thanks." She smiles at that, maybe at your accent, maybe at your girth, and then with her tray piled two high with cups and saucers, she walks away.

You pocket the bill from Bewleys thinking about tomorrow and the archives. There will be Irish mementos, you think, documents, a story that can be told: *I carried you through Dublin in my belly then brought you home to London to be born. We stayed at a small B&B on Kirwin Street and the woman, a Mrs. Donaghue, gave me a pail before bed so I could soak my feet. We walked the whole city in search of answers. You kicked up quite a fuss.*

But still you imagine your hands spread open and empty before the child. At least now there's the possibility of a gift: an album of information and faces, a whole genealogy and even that damn photo of your own father if you can shake out of your mum what's been done with it. The photo of Adam in the wingback has come out beautifully and everything about it indicates a kind of settled happiness, the implication of love. He may yet muster up the nerve to admit his affair to Victoria, and that might galvanize her into action. What if Victoria gave him up? Threw all his shirts, the contents of his sock drawer out the bedroom window? What will you do with him if he is yours for the taking? When everything is said and done, what can he finally provide?

Archives

The National Library is an intimidating building. The long stretch of front steps arrives at two huge wood doors. The early morning sun glitters off large panels of brass. You'd tried to freshen up after breakfast, had repowdered your face and applied a dab of lipstick. Your hair you'd rolled up in the semblance of a bun, and so far, except for that straggly brown bit that rests against your right cheek, it feels as though it hasn't fallen out. The best you've been able to do with your clothes is comfortable flats and knee-highs under a green short-sleeved dress, one that resembles a hot air balloon when you consider how amply you fill it out. You're carrying your cardigan in your arms along with your ratty tapestried day bag. But it all comes to naught in the archives. Everyone is seated at a desk, preoccupied, going about their business. Not one of the dozen heads in the room lifts up to note your effort, no one cares that your socks are falling down. They just pore over stacks of paper, notes covered in handwritten encryptions, text labelled with official-looking stamps.

The smell of toner from fresh photocopies mixes with the smell of musty old books; it itches your nose until you give a squeaky sneeze. Now you have their attention and you decide to sit down. The librarian brings the microfiche you've asked for and he wends it into the machine. Before you are church registries for the Galway area, each microfiche covering a span of some fifty years. You press "Forward" and watch the pages go, white rectangles of text zipping across the microfilm screen.

There is the feel of an old film about it, the clipped sound of the negative stretched and running between glass. You think of Chaplin and Adam just then, but get back to the task at hand, your Gran's notes set out beside you. After almost an hour, you see something, a thin scrawl, the name O'Keefe, a date and location. The pen you reach for slips in your hand.

Later, at Christchurch Cathedral, you sit on concrete steps and lean backwards, putting all your weight on your elbows. There is a view of the flower beds past the walkway; it's interrupted only by the odd pedestrian. Looking up, the sky is cluttered with arch and steeple, two buttresses that extend from the cathedral wall like limbs. You have your notes and some photocopies from the microfiche in your bag and for a minute you feel content here, as if this is the perfect place to bring a child into the world, all the solidity of architecture, stone pillars thicker and more stable than anything Adam has designed. And the time is probably near enough; the baby is punch boxing inside you. Using your muscles you try to signal back, but when you give a push you almost wet yourself. You resolve that it is best to wait, get home to Adam and family, the comfort of the familiar and mundane—your plaster ceiling complete with its cracks, the scratch of mice inside the walls.

You think of Charlotte and imagine her in a smart brown hat with a wide fancy brim and cream ribbons, fresh from the farm near London. "I'm going to him," she would have told her father. She would have gone up to her mother's room and kissed her softly on the cheek. "I'm going to James and we're to be married. That is all I have to say." Then the incident, the way her father must have pulled her by the neck over towards the sink, the cook standing in the corner, mutely watching Lottie's father shear off the girl's hair. Lottie would have boarded the next boat and set sail, maybe stopping in Dublin long enough to sit in the swirl of this cathedral's arches.

You imagine Lottie standing beside you on the step. Picture her magnificent in a long summer dress of linen, her hair cropped to shreds. "Have a sit," you say out loud and to your amazement she does. "Hello," you say, "hello." It is delightful and somewhat dangerous, you think, to be sitting alone in a strange city talking to the empty space beside you, but you continue nonetheless, feeling invigorated by the high sun and the aromatic breeze from the nearby flower beds.

"Nasturtiums," Lottie says.

You nod and she reaches out to take your hand.

"You're almost ready, then?" She raises an eyebrow and strokes the backs of your fingers.

"Tuesday, they say." Then you ask, "Will it hurt?" You imagine she would know.

"I think it's what you make of it."

She leans forward from the pillar, the sun casting her face in a warm yellow glow.

"And you?" you ask her, pressing your fingers into your temples and closing your eyes. "What did you make of it?"

Audibly she says "I, Emma, am what I have made of myself."

You feel a twinge and look down at the mound of your belly long enough to be distracted and when your thoughts of Charlotte return she is nowhere to be found. You can summon nothing more than the breeze. You had wanted her to stay. And you would like to be rid of the one loitering around in your body. You want him out, able to account for himself, make bubbly noises or conversation; breathing his own air, pounding his fists on something other than you. Soon enough it will be over.

Whatever you can make of it, you will. You will not spend your summers with your back pressed up against a wall, your thoughts directed at an empty doorway, the idea of Adam. You will not abandon your baby and head out into the world searching for the man you lost. These are choices, choices we make ourselves. Men and misery may have followed us all of our days but you are not entirely a product of previous generations. Start by heading back to the B&B. Tomorrow: Galway, an old plot of land and perhaps their graves. The papers sit securely in your bag. The wind is picking up, though. You remember Mrs. Donaghue saying over breakfast that a storm is coming on.

The Calm Before

Ponderous cows stand fat against the cut green fields. Suddenly everything is lucid. Meandering on a bus across the midriff of the country you work at relaxing your back muscles, all the while eyeing the countryside. This, you think, is somewhere, a rooted place. In comparison, Camden seems grotty and crowded, a dense display of overpopulated camaraderie, people spilling out of market stalls, fish and chips or other sundry purchases in hand. An amiable junkyard, a sort of purgatory for the underestablished. The bus dips down a slight hill then curves slowly right, nothing sudden, no big surprises. You whiz past a sign that reads Gaillimh, missing the numbers that tell you how far you have to go.

There was a wall where a woman waited and where one day, on the eighth anniversary of their marriage, her husband came sauntering along. He took her hand and begged forgiveness. That is the story the old man at O'Leary's abattoir tells you, saying, "Sure, but I remember the story well," then talking at length about the changes to the town, the tides of tourists that seem to have no end. He sends you over to a Morgan who sends you to Mrs. Magee. She gives you hot honey water and puts a cushion under your feet, finally sending you outside the city to young Tommy O'Keefe.

"He was some relation," the boy tells you, although at first he can't say for sure. Thinks on it then says, "Right, it was a great-uncle. Ack, but God knows I'm not the one to keep track." He's all of eighteen, stays alone while his father is North on business. "He'd know more but won't be back for the week." Self-conscious, he saunters through the living room and out the screen door. Takes you out back into the yard to a rotting knurled tree, names scratched and etched down into the bark. You trace the letters with your fingers, skin puckering into the nicked slats. He finds "James" for you and then, just under it, a second "James" in smaller hand. Beside that: "Lottie. Oct. 1924."

Tommy O'Keefe is mopping at his forehead while you look through the stack of pictures. He's just run back from the Spar and is offering you juice and pretzels; a boy having his best go at hospitality. You sort through faces you don't recognize, a wash of monochrome images. Somehow you think you'll know them.

"Do you know what love is?" you remember your mother asking. "And can you define it?" Here, at last, it is. A tall sturdy man sitting with his arms around a delicate-looking woman. A white blanket angling in from somewhere outside the photo. There's a picnic—evidence behind them of a plate, two blurred glasses, as if they'd just started to fall. Her hair is brown and wavy like your own, her eyes are similar to yours. Both James and Lottie are oblivious to the camera, as if the other person is the only one in the whole of the world who matters.

Accord

A great hunger drives us. We want to know things, emphatically, and we want to preserve what we know, as if it could be stored in a great bog and pulled out for analysis at any time. Take Lindow Man. *His hair was reddish, he'd had oats for lunch.* And there's more we can tell you. *This was his history, how long he lived, there was a small nick on his thumb. These, we believe, are the matters that haunt him.* And so, you wonder, what moment of your panic, of your coming-to-terms, will be retained? Will you always remember sitting in the dim light of this house, the curtains lifting into the living room from the open window, the moment you held this photo in your hand? So take this photo—a record in time. Take your palm and press it against a wedge of cut wood embellished on a tree. Claim your history with your hands.

You think: James did not disown Lottie. He had simply come to question what he knew, been forced to evaluate the possibility of something else—a life in the country, a life ruled by poverty, the remaining years without her. Maybe this is what Adam is doing: weighing out love of various kinds, coming to terms with a life that involves some kind of departure. He wills things for you in his wordless way, he wills you patience, as James must have prayed for Lottie's patience. He must have hoped every year that he'd see her again, even if he still wasn't ready.

On the phone from Belfast, Patrick O'Keefe tells you what he knows. His son paces back and forth beside your chair in the kitchen. In order to please his father, James did a bout of gun-running in Mayo. Spent nights burying munitions for the Irish Republican Brotherhood. He travelled the length of the country but came back to Galway again and again. Later he joined the war in France and after two months quietly left it, having seen enough to know. When he came back to Charlotte, she refused to let him out of her sight; they sometimes came to this house— James' brother's house—to visit the family. And that's as much as he knows.

You imagine her taking him back, memorizing every sleeping twinge, the manner in which he pursed his lips before speaking. She must have traced and retraced the hard lines that had come across his face in the years since she'd last seen him. You imagine she never laid judgement against him. O'Keefe said they started with a mare and that was all of her money. From London, her aunt sent letters on the progress of the child. Plans were made to set up a house and stable, bring the girl over.

A Book of Hours

Adam isn't making plans and you don't blame him. He is walking the fine line between dedication and departure; he's like the ticket-taker at the ramp before the plane takes off. He'll be at the door of your flat one evening and at home, tucking his children into bed, the next. And you don't want to lure him from them. Even in the early days you never envisioned that. Rather, you took Victoria out of the equation and imagined yourself in football stadiums and at the school play cheering the children on. This is not about one-upmanship and broken homes, and you hope Adam knows that. You only want your child to know he has a father who loves him, a father who did more than turn in the hospital corridor or pack his bags and leave without so much as a word.

There are a million moments with Adam that are worth keeping and you'll have them, even if he ultimately leaves. You could fill a volume full of books with these things, chapters like: "A Compendium of His Odd Expressions"; "His Varied Positions in Sleep"; "A List of Landmarks Visited"; "Quotes From His Ideology on Love."

The summer you first met, Adam said that love isn't malleable, that we aren't the masters of its construction. He said it like he thought love was something that reared its head and demanded you obey it. But still he took your hand as if to assure you that he could act of his own volition. You pulled Winston along, and the three of you walked along the canal towpath, scattering the pigeons.

What part of your life would you take back if you could? What moment, what hour, what day? Would it be the day you opened the desk drawer and noticed your father's photo missing, or the time you yelled at your mum that you didn't love her, that you wished she were dead? Would it be the morning of your baby's conception, that seemingly insignificant carnal hour? And would it make a difference anyway? Adam loves you and against your will you stupidly and idiotically love him. An hour, or a day, couldn't change it. You'd still be with him in the end.

The Storm

You take the photo with you. James and Lottie. Lottie is not like
you had imagined her, but softer, more feminine. Still, she looks
like a strong woman and her gaze is steady and fixed. It rests on
him. There is something of your mother in her, a solidity of
sorts, a solidity you strive for.

You try to get it straight in your mind, try to follow the events
that have led you here, but everything is too muddled. So you
stand at the bus stop in Galway with your day bag over your
arm, the pressure in the womb increasing. The weight of the
baby's body pushes against you in different places as if he is
shifting positions, getting ready to make way into the world.
When the Dublin bus arrives you set your back against the bus
seat, breathe in and out again. Sitting helps, but still, you're
aware that the thrust and push is lower than ever before. Make
way to the loo at the back of the bus, make way and hope the
driver hurries on.

There is a push against the abdomen and again a push, but
not what you'd think of as labour, according to what you've
read about such matters. Another push, as if the baby is getting
impatient. So here you are again at the pivotal moment. And you
think about the tube ride a month ago to Bayswater, to Adam,
about the agreements made, the filling out of bank forms.
Winston pulling at you with needs of his own and how all you
could do was write in your notebook *what is important*. How
you assumed then that you would know.

At the Dublin bus station you check your watch. It is 3:15

and there is, you think, a ferry out to Liverpool at just past five. You consider what you've left at the B&B because you'd intended to go back there, and realizing it is only a dress and nightie, toiletries, wet stockings hanging over the shower rod, you start out to O'Connell Street to hail a taxi. Please God, you think, let us make it to London, even if I have to go through contractions on the train, let this baby be born in the hospital. You remember the story of Clara's birth, how it happened after the stairwell fell in, the sounds of air raid sirens screaming above your grandmother's head. She counted their rotations, four hundred and sixty-two, later writing it down. This one is also demanding to be heard. Another wave rips through you. You'll never hear the end of it from your mum. Complications now and you'll never forgive yourself.

"Driver!" You push yourself into the back of the taxi, the man looking at you incredulously.

"Where to?"

"Dun Laoghaire please. For the ferry."

And off you speed through the traffic, the driver doing everything short of ride on the sidewalk. He lays on the horn and even leans his upper body out the window at an intersection, yelling, "Haul it, or this one's having a baby on me!" To which the lorry driver responds, "Up yours."

If this is the moment, then you should be prepared, but where were the preparations to begin with? Where were the secret all-girl clubs you could have joined, with their codes of honour, ethics, their written out best laid plans, the badges and medals? Where were the mystical women's groups that met in buildings marked "To Let" in Camden Town, the secrets of readiness relayed in whispers, favourite recipes traded, the pros and cons of disposable diapers fully discussed.

But this, you think, is fate. In the taxi to Dun Laoghaire, the driver rambles on about his two children, hair as red as the day, and you think you'd like to give it all up to fate, which just might be easier than getting your big, tired body out of the taxi-cab and rolling it onto the ferry. Fate, you guess, just might be your best friend. Fate holding you at arm's length, guiding you up the ferry ramp, handing over your boarding pass to the stocky steward. Fate looking over the bow and saying "water." Fate sitting you down in the lounge and making you cry, the shipload of possibility and complications having, at last, arrived.

You call your mother from the "ship to shore" when you feel calmer, tell her to gather up the interested parties and make for the hospital where you should be arriving in six or so hours. You instruct her to call Adam and to hang up if Victoria answers the phone. And she says she will call, although both of you know now that he isn't what really matters. "I love you, Em," she says it with strength and conviction, and standing by the purser's office on the ferry, your baby doing something like handstands in the womb, you know she really means it.

In This

In this photo are two lovers. James and Lottie. You look at the image of your great-grandparents while standing by the porthole in lounge B. Here are the smaller details of their lives. A gaze, the slightly awkward angle of her bad leg, a slope of shoulder, the thin band of a wedding ring. They were crossing on the ship Mercy, going back to London, this is what the older O'Keefe said; there was an accident in the boilers and everyone was called to the boats. The Irish Sea was a murky depth after all, an instrument in our failures. 1928. They and eight others drowned.

You choose to believe they were heading back to their daughter, that having at last sorted themselves out, their house and stable ready, they were set on retrieving her. *This,* they could have said, *is what we have to give you.* But in the end we simply arrive. Your trials and errors, false starts, run like a train from London to Norwich and into Dublin and the coast beyond. Your preparation barely evident—as if you could prepare at all—and so the result is this: the baby comes first, Adam can join you or he can stay away, finding those bits of himself that, when added up, fulfill him. There is only one direction now.

The ferry sails into Liverpool; the sky is darker here and more polluted. But celebrate: it's the industrial age that brought you safely home in a steel-hulled luxury hotel where the price of apples is uncanny but free soap bars abound in the loo. England, the home of industry where the world as we know it was born; our inheritance, then, is to keep busy, stand ready and be ever productive. Reinvent the textile mill, and restart the smelting factories at Coalbrookdale. All hands prepare for evolution: a woman has come home to give birth.

It's all in the breathing, you think. You are on the train at last and speeding through the countryside, the dimly lit trees and stations peeling by the windows in inspired dizziness. Or perhaps your perspective is skewed; you put your head down towards your knees, as close as ambition will get you, and wait for it to come.

The two boys in the seats across from you are curious but after you fail to directly entertain they go back to the plastic action figures making war on the hills of their knees. Somewhat shaken, it is your temple throbbing in time to the contractions that keeps you in line. Inhale, throb, exhale, throb and so it goes. And that is what they are—contractions. The awkward pivotal shift the baby had made is no longer apparent, which leads you to believe that he has given up basketball for diving. Pulling into Birmingham you head for the loo but halfway up the aisle your water breaks, soaking your tights, thin rivulets running down your thighs towards the carpet. Sit while you can, there will be plenty to do soon enough. "Miss," you address the mother of the two boys, "would you mind summoning the conductor?"

Letting Go

The train pulls into London and the crank of metal announces your arrival. The conductor escorts you down the steps into the arms of two ambulance attendants who heave you onto the gurney.

"Good evening Ma'am," one says.

"Do you have any pain?" says the other.

Your mother, who is pacing the hospital's admitting area, rushes alongside the stretcher when you arrive and she rants at you for a few inaudible minutes. By God she is angry, and that, you realize, is a surprising change so you smile up at her in the elevator to the labour room. She squeezes your hand until that hurts as much as the contractions.

"Adam?" you ask.

"I took a chance and left a message."

It's nothing like you thought it would be, having heard stories about your own birth. Your mother's pelvis a wishbone of sorts until it slowly worked itself back into place. On the one hand, you suppose, she was pulling for you, and on the other she was pulling for Henry William Westcott. The week she spent recovering in the hospital was about loss as much as anything. Her preparations were made with a cinch around her hips, the knowing looks of nurses. Unlike you, she could only make notes in order of importance, *the baby, the baby, the baby*, no room for *options* at all.

Adam is there in the last few minutes, unshaven, dishevelled, but he too is squeezing your hand and grinning like a maniac. You don't know whether to slap him or kiss him, so you clench your eyes against the possibilities, everything a wound coil that springs in waves of pain. "Push." The doctor calmly giving instructions. "And again." You feel the slick sheet underneath you, the cloth your mother dabs up against your forehead, Adam's finger gripped in the middle of your fist. You've bitten into your lip and can taste the blood. A surge, and then another. You curl your toes over until they cramp, think that there is no more pushing, you've done your best. And then an opening up, like being struck, given a great gashing wound. You see him. There he is.

"Emma," Adam says, "oh, Em, a boy," and that is it until they bring him up close to you. Already he's flailing about, his fists hitting this way and that. His mouth an open bellow. The baby who becomes everything—not options, not priorities, just fingers, toes and a small red face whose eyes are barely open to the world. Preparation behind you, he has arrived at last, and you know now, you can only pick up your bags, push Winston's leash up your arm, make ready and arrive with him. What else is there to do?

A c k n o w l e d g m e n t s

For their generosity and enthusiasm I am indebted to the follow-ing individuals: Jack Hodgins, Timothy Findley, Carolyn Swayze, my editor Lynn Henry, Michelle Benjamin, Patrick Lane, Lorna Crozier, David Grierson and Billeh Nickerson. Thanks also to my family, to Howard Anderson for the archives, to the wonderful folks at Raincoast Books and to the Popular Reading division at the Vancouver Public Library. Thanks especially to Kerry Syred Ohana and Angela McGoldrick for friendship that's spanned continents, and to rps who, years ago, placed more than a few good books in my hands.

Early versions of some of these stories first appeared in *Prism International*, *Grain* and *The Dalhousie Review*. Thank you to the editors for supporting my work.

Thanks to the British Columbia Arts Council for support in the form of funding. Heartfelt thanks to the Writing faculty and students at the University of Victoria where much of this manu-script was written, and to the MFA Creative Writing program at the University of British Columbia.

And finally, thanks to my husband Glenn, who keeps me sane and brings me immeasurable joy.

About the Author

Aislinn Hunter was born in Belleville, Ontario and moved to Dublin, Ireland for a few years before making her home in British Columbia. She recieved a BFA from the University of Victoria and an MFA from UBC. She has published widely in literary journals in Canada and abroad. She currently lives in Vancouver with her husband and their dog Fiddler.

Bright Lights from Polestar Book Publishers

Polestar takes pride in creating books that enrich our understanding of the world, and in introducing superb writers to discriminating readers.

FICTION

Stubborn Bones by Karen Smythe
"Karen Smythe brings to her fiction a combination of sharp intelligence and delicate sensibility. With a few deft strokes she manages, in these under-stated stories, to create a mood—lyrical and elegaic—that haunts the reader long after the book is finished." —Joan Givner
1-55192-364-5 • $21.95 CAN/$16.95 USA

Daughters are Forever by Lee Maracle
Maracle's new novel reinforces her status as one of the most important First Nations writers. A moving story about First Nations people in the modern world and the importance of courage, truth and reconciliation.
1-55192-410-2 • $21.95 CAN/$16.95 USA

diss/ed banded nation by David Nandi Odhiambo
"Thoroughly convincing in its evocation of young, rebellious, impoverished urban lives ... an immersion into a simmering stew of racial and cultural identities ..." —*The Globe and Mail*
1-896095-26-7 • $16.95 CAN/$13.95 USA

Pool-Hopping and Other Stories by Anne Fleming
Shortlisted for the Governor-General's Award, the Ethel Wilson Fiction Prize and the Danuta Gleed Award. "Fleming's evenhanded, sharp-eyed and often hilarious narratives traverse the frenzied chaos of urban life with ease and precision." —*The Georgia Straight*
1-896095-18-6 • $16.95 CAN/$13.95 USA

POETRY

Blue by George Elliott Clarke
Blue is black, profane, surly, damning, and unrelenting in its brilliance. George Elliott Clarke has written urgent and necessary poems about the experience of being black in North America.
1-55192-414-5 • $18.95 CAN/$13.95 USA

The Predicament of Or by Shani Mootoo
The author of the award-winning novel *Cereus Blooms at Night* turns her hand to poetry in a lively and nuanced exploration of desire, identity and personal exile.
1-55192-416-1 • $18.95 CAN/$13.95 USA